"Chelsey, you can't stay here. Eventually they'll figure out where we're located. The best way you can help me is to get to the cabin."

"I'm scared," she whispered.

"I know, but I'll keep diverting their attention until you're safe."

"And then you'll meet me there?"

"Yes. I need you to trust me on this. Once you're at the cabin, I can move quicker without worrying about your ability to follow me."

"Okay, I'll do it."

"Thank you." He couldn't hide his relief. "Here's how we're going to do this. The second I throw the rock, you're going to move, but stay on your belly, crawling like we did in order to get here, okay?"

She drew in a deep breath and nodded. "Yes."

"Each time I throw something, they're going to shoot. That's your cue to keep moving."

"Got it."

It wouldn't be easy for Chelsey to cover a hundred yards crawling on her hands and knees. But he was determined to give her every opportunity to get to safety.

Even if that meant sacrificing himself.

Laura Scott is a nurse by day and an author by night. She has always loved romance and read faith-based books by Grace Livingston Hill in her teenage years. She's thrilled to have published over twenty-five books for Love Inspired Suspense. She has two adult children and lives in Milwaukee, Wisconsin, with her husband of over thirty years. Please visit Laura at laurascottbooks.com, as she loves to hear from her readers.

Books by Laura Scott

Love Inspired Suspense

Justice Seekers

Soldier's Christmas Secrets
Guarded by the Soldier
Wyoming Mountain Escape

Callahan Confidential

Shielding His Christmas Witness
The Only Witness
Christmas Amnesia
Shattered Lullaby
Primary Suspect
Protecting His Secret Son

True Blue K-9 Unit: Brooklyn

Copycat Killer
True Blue K-9 Unit: Brooklyn Christmas
"Holiday Stalker"

Visit the Author Profile page at Harlequin.com for more titles.

WYOMING MOUNTAIN ESCAPE

LAURA SCOTT

LOVE INSPIRED SUSPENSE

INSPIRATIONAL ROMANCE

LOVE INSPIRED® SUSPENSE
INSPIRATIONAL ROMANCE

Recycling programs
for this product may
not exist in your area.

ISBN-13: 978-1-335-58115-0

Wyoming Mountain Escape

This edition published by arrangement with Harlequin Books S.A.

For questions and comments about the quality of this book, please contact us
at CustomerService@Harlequin.com.

Love Inspired
22 Adelaide St. West, 40th Floor
Toronto, Ontario M5H 4E3, Canada
www.Harlequin.com

Printed in U.S.A.

Now the God of hope fill you with all joy and peace
in believing, that ye may abound in hope,
through the power of the Holy Ghost.
–*Romans* 15:13

This book is dedicated to Kyle and Daniele Doberstein.

Congratulations on starting your new life together.
I wish you both peace, love and happiness.

ONE

Chelsey Robards walked out of the Teton Valley Hotel and approached the grassy knoll where her wedding guests waited. She paused at the front of the aisle, her stomach knotted with tension. Wearing a white gown, her veil trailing from a ring of flowers pinned in her curly golden-blond hair, she looked apprehensively at Brett Thompson, her long-time friend and soon-to-be-husband. Brett smiled encouragingly from his position near the right side of an arched lattice decorated with Wyoming wildflowers—the place they'd chosen to exchange their vows. Snow-covered Tetons, a section of the majestic Rocky Mountains, loomed behind Brett, creating a picture-perfect scene. Bars from

"The Wedding March" began to play, but her feet refused to move.

This is a terrible mistake.

Chelsey had ignored the lingering doubts she'd experienced over the past week. The doubts had grown more pronounced when Duncan O'Hare, her and Brett's childhood friend, had arrived to fulfill his role as best man. Chelsey's friend and assistant manager, Trish Novak, was standing in as her maid of honor. Seeing Brett and Duncan together reinforced Chelsey's doubts.

She couldn't do this. Marrying Brett was a mistake. How had she let it go this far? She'd known Brett and Duncan from childhood, until her parents had moved to Wyoming the summer after her freshman year of high school. She loved Brett, but she understood now that she loved him as a friend.

Not a husband.

The song continued, her guests waiting expectantly. What should she do? She couldn't embarrass Brett by refusing to marry him in front of their friends and relatives.

Duncan's intense dark gaze caught her eye, his expression full of concern as if he sensed her inner turmoil. Drawing strength from Duncan, she forced herself to take the first step. And another.

The closer she came to the arched lattice where Brett waited, the more her stomach twisted painfully. She swallowed against the urge to throw up. Despite the sunlight overhead, she felt cold to the bone.

As she approached her husband-to-be, she abruptly stopped, unable to take that final step toward Brett. Every eye from those seated in the grassy knoll was glued to her and it was all she could do not to turn and run away as fast as her white ballet slippers would take her.

Brett's smile never faltered. He waited patiently, having no idea how she felt. In contrast, Duncan's dark brown gaze was serious, and she knew she wasn't fooling him.

Not the way she'd fooled everyone else.

The song was winding down and she couldn't postpone the inevitable any longer. She had to do this, even if it meant telling Brett afterward that she wanted an annulment. They could return the gifts and walk away as if this never happened.

Couldn't they?

A sharp crack ripped through the air. It took a minute for her to notice the red spot blooming on Brett's white shirt as he staggered backward.

"Get down!" Duncan lurched forward, grabbed her arm and dragged her away from Brett who'd crumpled to the ground.

He'd been shot!

Screams and bedlam broke out around them, the wedding guests scattering like mice, but Duncan didn't let go of her hand. He dragged her away from the area, down the hill toward the wooded mountainside.

It was difficult to comprehend what had just happened. "Wait! We need to go back to Brett! He's been shot!"

"He's gone, Chelsey, but the shooter is

still out there, somewhere. We need to keep moving."

No! This couldn't be happening! Brett! There wasn't time to think, to truly comprehend. She followed in Duncan's wake. Her bridal gown was long, and she kept tripping over the hem, the train picking up leaves and sticks as they raced for cover.

"But—I don't understand." Her mind was a chaotic, emotional mess. She didn't want to marry Brett, but she didn't want him *dead*. She loved him. He was a good friend. *Dear Lord in heaven, what is going on?* This didn't make any sense. Who would shoot him? On their wedding day?

And why?

"Come on." Duncan tugged on her hand, steering her toward a cluster of trees. It was mid-June and her white gown would be glaringly obvious against the green foliage.

"But—" Another loud crack echoed

around them and Duncan yanked her down and behind the base of a large tree.

"We need someplace to hide." Duncan's voice was calm, as if running from gunfire was an everyday occurrence.

"My gown..." Her teeth began to chatter as if she were freezing cold. "W-we'll be t-too noticeable."

"It's okay, I'll protect you." Duncan's deep voice was ridiculously reassuring, even though she had no idea who he was protecting her from. He swept his gaze around the area, then gestured to the left. "This way."

She wasn't in a position to argue. He stood and helped her up, steering her toward another large tree. The air had fallen silent, and she hoped, prayed the shooter had cut and run.

They continued their zigzag pattern using the various trees and rocks for cover, moving from one place to the next. At some level she realized Duncan was taking them deeper into the woods and up the mountain. Her ballet slippers weren't designed for this kind of rugged terrain, and she could feel every rock and stick poking at the soles of her feet.

Duncan didn't let up his aggressive pace, moving swiftly and silently through the woods. She risked a glance over her shoulder. They'd gone so far that she could barely see the grassy knoll or the lattice arch. Only a hint of the log cabin frame of the Teton Valley Hotel was visible through the trees.

It was as if all evidence of her wedding had vanished.

A searing guilt stabbed deep. Was this somehow her fault? That her deep desire to avoid marrying Brett had caused this to happen? No, that didn't make any sense, but she still couldn't shake the shroud of guilt.

Poor Brett. No one deserved to die. To be shot in the chest at his own wedding. He'd always been nice and kind to her, especially when they reunited just a few months ago at her mother's funeral.

Maybe it was the shock of losing her mother that had caused her to turn to Brett for comfort. That made her accept his surprising proposal. At first she'd felt complete, as if this was what God wanted—for her to move on with her own life.

Until the doubts began to creep in. Growing worse as the big day approached.

Her veil caught on a low-hanging tree branch. Tears sprang to her eyes as the flowered headpiece was yanked from her hair.

"Are you okay?" Duncan's keen gaze didn't miss a thing.

She nodded, even though she was far from okay.

She'd never be okay again.

They continued their mountain trek until she could barely move. Finally, Duncan stopped behind an outcropping of boulders.

"We'll rest here for a bit."

She dropped to the ground where she stood, pulling up the ragged, dirty hem of her gown to peer at her feet. The white ballet slippers were brown and already beginning to split at the seams. Full of despair, she kept remembering the blood-stain growing in the center of Brett's white shirt directly over his heart. Yet the horrific memory didn't bring her to tears. Her dear friend, the man she'd promised to marry, was dead. Brutally shot at their wedding.

Why wasn't she sobbing buckets of tears?

"Chelsey, look at me." Duncan's voice penetrated her internal thoughts. She lifted her head to look up at him. "I need to find fresh water for us to drink, or we'll become severely dehydrated out here. Will you wait here? Water is trickling nearby, but I'm not sure exactly where it is."

Dehydration? Was that why she couldn't cry? At least that made sense, a bit of logic in a world that had suddenly turned upside down. "I'll wait." The words came out as a hoarse croak.

Duncan's hand gently squeezed her shoulder. "I'll be back very soon."

She nodded again, because frankly she didn't have a choice. Now that she was sitting on the ground, she didn't have the strength to go on. Not that sitting on the mountain all night held any appeal.

Duncan still wore his light gray tux and white shirt. His dark blue boutonniere had been lost along the way. Other than his chocolate-brown hair being damp with sweat, he didn't show any sign of exertion. And when he moved out of her line of vision, her chest tightened with panic.

"Duncan, wait!" Her earlier exhaustion vanished. She struggled to her feet, unwilling to be left alone.

He quickly returned his dark gaze full of concern. "Easy, Chelsey, you're going to be fine. We're safe."

"How do you know? What if the gunman followed us?"

"Based on the trajectory of the bullet, I believe he was on the roof of the hotel when he shot Brett. There's no way he could have followed us through the woods." Duncan sat beside her wrapping his arm around her shoulders. "We're going to be fine, Chelsey. We'll get through this."

She leaned against him, burrowing her face in the hollow of his shoulder. Maybe it was wrong to seek comfort in Duncan's arms so soon after losing Brett, but she couldn't seem to help herself.

If anyone could get her out of this mess alive and in one piece, it was Duncan O'Hare.

Duncan cradled Chelsey close, inwardly reeling from the brutal slaying of Brett Thompson.

What in the world had his old buddy gotten involved in?

The hit had been done by a professional, there was no doubt about that. Chilling to realize just how close he'd come to losing Chelsey, too.

The second shot had been meant for her. It was the only explanation. Otherwise, why hadn't the shooter taken off, disappearing amid the chaos?

Duncan had been in Jackson, Wyoming, for only five days, but from the moment he'd arrived, he'd sensed there was something going on with Brett.

The guy had been skittish, constantly looking over his shoulder, as if expecting someone to come up and grab him from behind. When Duncan had pressed him for information, Brett had shrugged off his concerns, focusing instead on how fortunate he was to have Chelsey as his fiancée. That he couldn't wait to marry her.

Now Brett was dead. Shot at his own wedding. Duncan's heart ached for what Chelsey had lost today. Not just a friend but her soon-to-be husband. He didn't blame her for falling apart.

Chelsey stirred in his embrace and he reluctantly loosened his grip. "Better?"

She nodded and pushed a strand of her wavy golden-blond hair from her cheek. "I'm sorry to break down like that."

"Hey, you're entitled after everything you've been through. I'm so sorry about Brett. I know the reality probably hasn't hit you yet, but I'm here for you, when it does."

She stared down at the ground for a long moment. "Thanks."

He glanced around. "I really need to find us water and shelter."

"My shoes are about to fall apart." She gestured to her mud-stained slipper-like shoes. "I'm not sure they'll hold up to more hiking."

The thought of her being barefoot concerned him. He lightly touched her bedraggled wedding gown. She'd looked so amazingly beautiful as she'd come toward Brett, but the poor dress had taken a beating during their mad dash through the woods. "I have a pocketknife. I think we should rip strips off your gown and wrap them around your feet."

"That might work." She didn't look upset at the thought of destroying her gown. Not that it was salvageable at this point anyway.

"Here." He dug the penknife out of his pocket and handed it to her. "Work on that while I'm gone."

She took the knife and picked up her voluminous skirt. Without hesitation, she sliced through the fabric and began sawing back and forth, creating the strips he'd suggested.

He eased to his feet and hurried off toward the sound of trickling water. The Tetons had snowcapped peaks even in June and he knew much of the water was melted snow. Pure enough, he hoped, that they wouldn't get sick.

Once he'd secured a water source, he could focus on a shelter and building a fire. Thankfully, his time in the army and being deployed overseas to serve in Afghanistan had provided the survival skills he needed to keep them safe.

The water wasn't far, a couple of yards and he stretched out on the ground, lowering his mouth to the stream to take a drink. They hadn't climbed up as much as they'd headed west, but it wouldn't take long for them to feel the change in altitude. Keeping well hydrated was critical.

Now all he needed was a way to carry the water back to Chelsey. Too bad they hadn't gone on the run with a water bottle. He stripped off the jacket of his tux and examined the pockets. They were a blend of polyester and cotton—not waterproof by any means, but it was possible they'd hold enough water for her to take a few sips.

After filling the pocket with water, he quickly carried it back to where Chelsey waited. The water seeped from the seams but remained halfway full by the time he offered it to her.

She eagerly drank, looking disappointed when it was gone.

"I'll get more," he promised. "But it would be easier if you could walk over there. It's not far."

"I only have two strips cut so far." She held up her work.

"Here, let me wrap these around your feet—that should hold for now. We can cut more later."

The strips helped to hold the flimsy shoes in place. He helped her stand and showed her the way to the brook. Once she'd taken her fill of water, she sat back with a sigh. "I didn't realize how thirsty I was."

He nodded, glancing around the area. "I need to find us shelter for the night."

"For the night?" Her voice rose in alarm. "We're staying out here all night?"

"Chelsey, we don't have another option. It's already eighteen hundred hours. I mean, six o'clock in the evening. Even with daylight savings time, the sun will be hidden behind the mountains soon. It will be dark here in the forest—we can't risk hiking at night."

"Why can't we go back to the hotel? I'm sure it's safe, the gunman is probably already under arrest."

He wasn't at all convinced. "Remember the second gunshot we heard?" When she nodded, he said gently, "Who do you think they were shooting at, considering Brett was already dead from being shot in the heart?"

She opened her mouth, then closed it again. After a long moment her voice came out in a squeaky tone. "Me? You think he was shooting at me?"

He hated upsetting her, but she needed to understand the scope of what they were dealing with. He glanced around again and gestured to the right. "I think that might be a small cave in the side of the mountain. I'm going to take a quick look."

This time, she didn't protest, clearly

reeling from the idea that someone had just tried to kill her.

The cave was more of a shallow curvature in the rock. It wasn't much. In fact, he didn't think both of them would fit sitting together within the indentation. But Chelsey was slim and petite. She could use it and he would sit outside the opening, keeping the fire going.

He returned to get Chelsey, who took another long drink of water before following him to the shelter. She didn't look impressed but sank down and leaned against the rocky wall anyway.

Scouting the area for firewood didn't take long, and soon he had a nice pile of logs and kindling. He didn't have a lighter so he used a flint rock and dried sticks, a trick the army had taught him, to create a spark. A bit of fabric from Chelsey's dress helped.

The spark turned into a flame. Lightly blowing on the small flame, he added one twig, then another, nurturing the flame into a full-blown fire. When he was satisfied it was large enough, he added a log and scooted back to sit close to Chelsey.

"Are you hungry?" He glanced at her.

She shivered. "No. I can't eat."

He understood she felt that way now, but they'd be hungry by morning. The body had a way of overriding grief to sustain basic needs. What was left of the sunlight was already fading and hunting in the dark wouldn't work, even if he had something to hunt with other than his penknife, which he didn't.

There was no point in thinking about food now. Tomorrow he'd need to come up with another plan.

What that would entail, he had no clue.

"Take my jacket." He tucked the edges of his tux around her shoulders. "The rock will be cold. Better that you stretch out on the ground instead."

"Okay." She did as he suggested, looking like a waif in her dirty and ripped wedding gown, wrapped in his tux. There was a long silence as they watched the fire. The flickering flames were mesmerizing, but now that he'd secured the basics of their survival needs, he wanted to understand exactly what had gone down earlier that evening.

"What was Brett involved in?"

She turned to stare up at him blankly. "What do you mean?"

"Brett must have been involved in something dangerous. Do you know anything about this new job he was all excited about? Something about working protection detail for a wealthy rancher who lived near the hotel?"

Her beautiful blue eyes crinkled with confusion. "What wealthy rancher? Brett worked as a project manager for Coyote Creek Construction. They construct businesses and residential homes. I don't know anything about Brett's alleged job of protecting a wealthy rancher."

He wrinkled his brow in confusion.

"How long has he been working for Coyote Creek Construction?"

"I'm not sure, maybe a couple of years? Why would he tell you some weird story about a new job working for a rancher? Especially a wealthy one? The only rancher we know is Elroy Lansing, and he certainly doesn't need protection from what I know. Frankly, his ranch has been going downhill the past few years—rumor has it he's selling land to anyone offering a cash deal."

No wealthy rancher needing protection? It didn't make any sense. Brett had obviously lied about his job, either to him or to Chelsey. And the more important question was, why? There was no reason, especially if he had a job working as a project manager for a construction company.

What secret was Brett covering up?

Whatever it was, it had likely gotten him killed.

And worse, put Chelsey in harm's way.

TWO

Lying on the ground wrapped in Duncan's jacket and watching the flickering flames dancing amid the kindling was surreal. The peace and tranquility were at direct odds with the horrifying way her wedding had ended, even before it had begun.

Chelsey had lived in Wyoming for twelve years, so it wasn't as if she'd never camped outside. She had, but never in a wedding dress. And never with Duncan determined to look after her.

It seemed wrong to be resting here, somewhat relaxed, when Brett was dead. Maybe it was a sign that her body couldn't tolerate any more stress.

The week leading up to the wedding

had been bad enough, wrestling with her doubts. Now all she felt was a blunt dullness. A resignation that she couldn't go back and change the past.

Brett was gone. It was difficult to wrap her mind around it. Duncan was right to explain how the reality of losing him hadn't hit her yet.

If only she'd explained to Brett how she was feeling before today. Maybe if she'd asked him to call off the ceremony, he'd still be alive. Mad and upset with her, yes, but alive.

Duncan's questions about Brett's job disturbed her. Why would Brett make up a story about protecting a wealthy rancher? Did he feel the need to be viewed by Duncan as more important than he really was? She remembered how Brett had planned to follow in Duncan's footsteps in joining the army, but his asthma diagnosis had made him ineligible to serve.

Was that what his bizarre story was about? Feeling better about himself?

They'd never know. Her chest tightened painfully. It was inconceivable that Brett was involved in something that had gotten him killed. Maybe this was nothing more than a case of mistaken identity.

But if so, why shoot at her?

The temperature dropped, making her shiver. Duncan must have noticed because he scooted closer. "Keeping close will help us both retain body heat."

She moved until her body was partially wrapped around his. Duncan's warmth was a balm to her fear and worry.

Trust in God. Wasn't that what her church pastor had taught them? She shied away from the thought. Concern over breaking her commitment to Brett had been something she'd wrestled with. She couldn't imagine what Pastor Rick would have said if she'd told him she needed to break off her engagement and cancel the wedding.

Had the local police been called? Were there men and women out there right now searching for the gunman? As well as for her and Duncan? It would make sense that they would be, especially as they were both witnesses.

Unless there was something she was missing.

It hit her suddenly, with the force of a brick to her abdomen, that she might be a suspect in Brett's murder. There was no motive, unless someone with Duncan's intuition had figured out that she had changed her mind about marrying him.

Not that it was really a motive. Killing him was a drastic measure when they could just as easily get an annulment. Yet who else would want him dead?

She had no idea. The thought of being a suspect in murdering Brett in cold blood was sickening.

"Relax, Chelsey. I can feel waves of tension radiating off you. Try to get some sleep."

It was quiet, other than the usual night sounds of the forest, but it wasn't that comfortable that she would be able to sleep. Drawing in a deep breath she tried to relax. To let go of the tension.

"You knew I was having doubts about getting married, didn't you?" The stark question popped out of her mouth before she could think about it.

Duncan didn't respond for several seconds. "You didn't look like a happy bride coming down the aisle. In fact, I was afraid you were going to be ill."

His intuition had been right on and explained the concerned way he'd been looking at her.

"Did Brett do something to upset you?" he asked.

"No." Honestly, it would have been easier if he had. But Brett was a nice and decent guy. She was the one with the issues, not him.

"Then what was bothering you?" Duncan's deep, husky voice made her shiver. It was crazy to be this aware of him. "Why were you having second thoughts?"

She couldn't tell him that seeing Duncan again had rekindled feelings she'd thought were long gone. How in that moment, she'd understood that she loved Brett as a friend and not as a husband.

"My mother died three months ago."

Duncan shifted ever so slightly, looking down at her. "I'm sorry to hear that. Your mom was a wonderful lady."

"After my father passed away two years ago, my mom and I became very close. Her death made me feel as if I was lost at sea without a boat or even a life preserver. When Brett came to the funeral, it was as if I'd been given a piece of my childhood back. One I didn't want to let go."

"I can see that."

Duncan's acceptance of her failures made her want to scream in frustration. Instead, she took a breath and continued to explain. "We began dating. It was so wonderful to have him here. His job was primarily based in Cheyenne and required him to travel a lot, so we made the most of the time we had together. When he proposed..." her voice trailed off. The memory was not a happy one. "I wasn't expecting it. I said yes, because he was beaming with excitement. And it wasn't that I didn't love and care about him."

"Marriage is a big step. It's understandable that you would have second thoughts."

"Stop making excuses for me." Her tone was sharp and she pushed herself upright into a sitting position. "I should have figured out that my caring about him was different from being in love with him. And now he's dead! Gone forever. And it's all my fault."

Tears pricked her eyes, but they came from a deep well of guilt.

"That's not true, Chelsey. His death isn't your fault."

"It is!" Why was Duncan being so stubborn? "If I'd called off the wedding ahead of time, the way I should have, none of this would have happened."

"Not in the same way it did, no. But if Brett was involved in something he shouldn't be, there would have been an attempt to get him another time. And don't forget, you were a target, too. If you hadn't walked down the aisle today, you may have been killed along with him in another location. I'm glad your life was spared."

She peered at him, trying to make out the expression on his face in the firelight. "You really believe that."

"Yeah, I do. That second shot wasn't an accident or a mistake. We were running away from the scene, which must have caught the shooter off guard. He probably expected you to go to Brett, giving him the perfect second shot. Instead, we took off, causing him to recalibrate his aim for the distance and our movements."

He spoke as if he knew exactly what the shooter had been thinking. "You're scaring me."

"I'm sorry." He didn't sound sorry. "But

you need to understand why we need to keep moving. Why we can't simply go back to the hotel. There's no way for us to know friend from foe."

His tone was so rational and reasonable in the face of this insanity.

If Duncan was right, and she was in danger, then he was the only thing standing between her and the shooter.

She owed Duncan her life and trusted him to keep her safe.

Duncan was grateful when Chelsey finally stretched back out on the ground beside him. He waited for her muscles to relax enough that she might be able to get some sleep.

Her statements about how she'd become engaged to Brett had surprised him. It made sense given the fact that things had happened so quickly after her mother had died.

Seeing Chelsey again after all these years had reminded him of how much he'd liked her. They were only young teenagers back then, so there was nothing serious that had ever transpired between them, but he'd always admired her. She'd been smart, beautiful and funny. He'd been upset that her parents had moved from Wisconsin to Wyoming to take over her grandparents' hotel. It felt as if she lived on the other end of the planet—that's how far apart those miles had seemed.

He and Brett had gone out to visit her one summer after graduating from high school. They'd had fun, but it wasn't as if there were dozens of job opportunities out there. Duncan had plans to join the army, while Brett had wanted to go to college in Chicago. They'd left Chelsey behind, promising to visit again, but they hadn't followed through.

Or at least, he hadn't followed through with visiting her. Obviously, Brett had come to Wyoming and had taken a job with the Coyote Creek Construction company.

Had his old friend done that as a way to be close to Chelsey? Probably.

When Duncan had come out for the wedding, he'd learned that Chelsey's parents had inherited the Teton Valley Hotel which had been in the family for several generations. The hotel likely belonged to Chelsey now, after the death of her mother. According to Brett, Chelsey loved playing the hostess to her guests and the hotel business was going well.

Then privately, Brett had claimed to have a new job that would enable him to live here in the valley with Chelsey. It had struck him as odd to hear that Chelsey hadn't known anything about it.

Too many things that didn't add up. As a former soldier and current cop with the Milwaukee Police Department, Duncan trusted his ability to keep Chelsey safe, but he also had a driving need to solve the puzzle of Brett's murder—and to uncover the reason Chelsey was in danger. Because he firmly believed the shooter wasn't finished with his plan. No doubt, the shooter would consider Chelsey a loose end.

Duncan added another log to the fire, then took a few minutes to rub dirt over his white shirt and light gray slacks. When he'd camouflaged himself as much as possible, he stretched out alongside Chelsey. He wanted to pull her into his arms but knew it was inappropriate. Instead, he edged as close as he dared to share his body heat.

As a former special ops soldier, Duncan knew how to rest while keeping his sixth sense on alert for a sign of the enemy. After his deployment, he'd had trouble sleeping and working as a police officer didn't help. Milwaukee had a high crime rate—not nearly as bad as Los Angeles or Chicago, but bad enough that he remained on high alert at all times.

Being in the mountains of Wyoming actually felt a little safer to him. It offered more hiding places than the urban environment of Milwaukee ever could. And was not nearly as dangerous as being in the mountains of Afghanistan.

He thought about his dad, Ian O'Hare, and his sister, Shayla Callahan, who had married her high school sweetheart, Mike Callahan. It would be nice to have the Callahans with him now, covering his back, but they were far away. As were Hawk and Ryker, his special ops army buddies.

Never in a million years did he expect to run into trouble in Jackson, Wyoming, of all places. That standing up for Brett and Chelsey's wedding would end up in a shooting that would send him and Chelsey running from gunfire.

If he'd known, he would have brought Ryker, Hawk or any of the Callahans along with him. The idea of calling his friends made him realize he had his cell phone in his pocket. Without disturbing Chelsey, he shifted enough to pull out his phone.

The bright light of the screen hurt his eyes, and he had to look away, giving his eyes time to adjust. But his hope deflated when he saw the tiny words along the top of the phone.

No service.

It figured. The Teton mountains were beautiful, but they didn't make for good cell reception. He shut down the phone to preserve the battery, since there was only thirty percent of a charge remaining, and slid the device back in his pocket.

A satellite phone would be handy right about now. Along with a hunting rifle. A bigger knife. And a few water bottles.

While he was at it, why didn't he ask for world peace and the solution to world hunger? The items he longed for were just as far out of reach.

He shook off the despair and focused on next steps. If he was alone, he wouldn't be so concerned. He'd survived and thrived under worse conditions.

Having Chelsey along increased the risk. Not just because she was wearing a wedding dress that stood out like a sore thumb, but because she wasn't used to roughing it in the woods.

They needed to rest until daylight, drink more water and find some sort of food source, not to mention going on the move to find another shelter.

Was he wrong to avoid returning to the hotel? It might be safe if there were enough cops hanging around. Chelsey had a point about the shooter being long gone.

Yet his gut screamed at him to keep Chelsey hidden. At least for a couple of days. Although how he'd manage to find out who the shooter was while stealthily moving along the mountainside was a good question.

He must have dozed because a strange rustling off in the distance jarred him awake. Easing away from Chelsey, he sat up, peering through the darkness. Wild animals were not uncommon, especially deer, elk, moose and bears.

Straining to listen, he tried to distinguish between the normal sounds of the night. The fire was nice and warm, but it was also a beacon to anyone who might be out there searching for them.

The embers glowed red hot, but instead of adding wood, he kicked dirt over the fire, putting it out.

In minutes they were surrounded in darkness, only slivers of light from the moon shining through the trees offering relief.

The silence stretched in a way that was abnormal. The tiny hairs on the back of his neck lifted in warning. He desperately wished he had a decent weapon on hand but hadn't anticipated needing one at a wedding.

Since the penknife was all he had, he opened the blade and clutched it lightly in his right hand, keeping himself positioned in front of Chelsey. He wanted to go on the move, to get as far away from here as possible, but knew her dress would hinder their ability to make a clean getaway.

Better to stand his ground, taking out

the enemy if that was the source of the rustling. He'd prefer any other animal to the shooter, except maybe a bear.

"Duncan? I'm cold."

Chelsey's plaintive tone sounded as loud as a scream ripping through the night. "Shh," he whispered, without taking his gaze from the wooded area surrounding them.

He was close enough to feel her go tense. "What's out there?"

"Don't talk." He bent down to put his mouth near her ear, in an effort to keep his voice as quiet as possible. "Scoot back into the crevasse as far as you can."

There was a slight rustling from her dress as she did as he'd asked.

He thought about his phone, and quickly pulled it out of his pocket. He didn't turn it on—the light would betray their location—but pressed the device into her hands. He didn't say anything but didn't need to. Chelsey was smart and would know without being told to use the phone as a way to get out of here if something happened to him.

Of course, she'd have to hike to a location where there was cell reception first.

Duncan straightened and widened his stance. He held the penknife in a loose grip, keeping the blade hidden at his side.

There was no doubt that he'd give his life to protect Chelsey's. Whoever was out there would have to kill him in order to get to her.

A familiar calm came over him, reminding him of his days in Afghanistan. He couldn't go into battle distracted, so he cleared his mind, focusing on the sounds and scents around him.

He heard the rustling sound again and he pinpointed it as coming from his left. He debated switching the blade to his left hand. He'd been taught to fight with either hand, even though his right was his dominant one. Since he hadn't been practicing the way he should have, he decided to keep the knife in his right hand, hoping the intruder wouldn't expect him to have a weapon and that he could use the element of surprise to his advantage.

Minutes passed with agonizing slowness, but the longer Duncan stood there, the more convinced he was that someone was out there. Animals didn't move with the pattern he was hearing. First rustling, then silence. Rustling, then more silence.

When he caught a glimpse of movement, he knew the intruder was close. He hoped and prayed that the dirt he'd smeared over his light clothes was enough to hide him. When a burst of movement came directly toward him, he was ready.

The man didn't appear to have a gun which gave Duncan a bit of hope. He waited until the guy was close before using the knife.

A burst of light came from behind him, blinding the assailant. The man lifted his arm in an attempt to block the light, giving Duncan the precious seconds he needed to take him down. They hit the solid earth with a thud. They rolled for a couple of feet, each vying for the upper hand.

But the guy wasn't about to give up so easily. It didn't take long for Duncan to realize he was in a brutal fight for his life.

One he didn't dare lose.

THREE

Chelsey watched in horror as Duncan and a man wearing black wrestled on the ground. The light of Duncan's cell phone glinted off something shiny and her heart squeezed as she realized it was a knife.

Duncan's knife? It looked bigger than she remembered and realized with a sick sense of dread the man in black must have one, too.

Their grunts and groans as they struggled were difficult to watch. Yet despite how much she wanted to, she couldn't tear her gaze away. The more they struggled, the more she realized they were evenly matched. She couldn't just stand here, she needed to help. To do something.

Her gaze landed on the pile of logs Duncan had gathered for their fire. Reaching for the biggest and heaviest one, she picked it up and took a step toward the fighting men.

Using Duncan's phone as a flashlight, she waited until the man in black was on top of Duncan before making her move. She had to be careful not to blind Duncan as the men fought to have the upper hand. She held her breath and brought the log down on the side of his head with all her strength. A loud whack echoed through the night.

The man groaned and must have loosened his grip, because Duncan flipped him over and quickly disarmed him. Looming over him, Duncan held the man's larger knife at his throat.

"Who are you?"

The man's eyes were closed, his entire body limp as if he were unconscious.

Her stomach lurched. She put a hand to her mouth. Oh no! Had she killed him?

"Chelsey? Get me a couple of those strips we cut from your dress."

Duncan's hoarse voice spurred her into action. She tossed the log back on the pile with distaste and went over to where they'd cut several strips off her dress to use as extra protection for her feet.

She brought them to Duncan and watched as he quickly bound the man's wrists and ankles.

"He's not dead?" Her voice came out in a hoarse whisper.

"No, just out cold." Duncan was breathing heavily as he glanced up at her. "Thanks."

She gave a shaky nod, relieved that she'd been able to help. "Now what?"

Duncan let out a sigh. He patted the man down. Lifting the man's slacks, she could see a gun strapped to his ankle. Duncan took the weapon along with the ankle holster and picked up the man's larger knife, with a grim satisfaction. "We need to move."

"Move where?" She didn't understand what he was saying. "I thought hiking at night was too dangerous?"

"It is." Duncan rose to his feet, grimacing a bit as if he were in pain. "But we don't have a choice. This guy is a professional. No ID, nothing to indicate who he's working for. We can't assume that he's alone, there could be others out there."

"Others?" She didn't like the sound of that and moved closer to Duncan while throwing a furtive glance over her shoulder. There was nothing to see in the inky darkness, yet she could easily imagine someone hiding out there. "Wouldn't anyone working with him have rushed forward to help once you began to struggle?"

"Maybe. Or maybe they've spread out to cover more ground, no way to know for sure."

She felt as if she'd been dropped in an alternate universe. She managed a family hotel, a place were nice people came to celebrate a birthday or their anniversary—not a place where men dressed in black came out of the darkness, searching for her with the intent to kill.

Was Duncan right? Had Brett somehow gotten involved in something sinister? As much as it was difficult to imagine, it was also the only thing that made sense.

And she couldn't help thinking about the crazy story he'd told Duncan about being hired as protection duty for a nearby rancher.

Was Elroy Lansing a part of this? As the only rancher in the immediate area, he must have been the one Brett was talking about.

"Let's go." Duncan took her arm. "We need to move."

"But—are we going to leave him here?" She glanced doubtfully at the unconscious man. "What if wild animals find him?"

"I'm sorry, but we have to. I told you, I don't think he's on the mountain alone. His team will find him before the wild animals get to him. Trust me, we need to be long gone when they do."

She couldn't argue his logic. "All right."

"First we'll wrap your feet." Duncan gestured for her to sit, and took several moments wrapping her feet in the remaining strips. Then he handed her the last one. "I need you to wrap this around my arm."

"Your arm?" She frowned, taking in his mud-stained shirt. "You're hurt?"

"It's a minor cut. But I don't want to leave a blood trail for anyone to follow." As he spoke, he stripped off his filthy shirt and turned so that she could see his arm. There was a three-inch cut on his bicep, oozing blood.

"It's going to get infected." First the dirty shirt, and now a strip from her gown.

"It will be fine for now." Duncan's tone was calm. "Just do your best."

Swallowing hard, she took the last strip from her dress and wrapped it around the wound, tucking the end over into itself to help keep it in place. His skin was warm to the touch, making her shiver with awareness.

Stop it. She gave herself a mental shake. What kind of woman lost her groom-to-be in a horrific murder and then noticed another man? A terrible woman. It was wrong on so many levels. She must be losing her grip on reality. This must be a weird reaction to the violence around her.

Duncan was an old childhood friend, like Brett. Nothing more.

"Okay, let's go." Duncan shrugged back into his shirt, helped her put his jacket back on, then took her hand.

"Where?" She tripped over a rock and might have fallen if he hadn't held her up.

For several long moments he didn't respond. He led the way without the aid of his phone flashlight app. She understood he was trying to preserve the phone battery, but that wouldn't matter much if they fell on their faces and ended up rolling like fallen logs down the mountain.

When they were far enough away from

their makeshift camp, he lowered his voice and spoke in a whisper as if worried the man they'd left unconscious and bound might be able to hear. "Up the mountain."

Up? Was he joking? She couldn't climb a mountain in the darkness.

In a wedding dress.

Yet that's exactly what she did. It was slow going, especially because of her lack of decent footwear. Duncan took his time, choosing their path carefully. She followed on his heels, doing her best to step where he did, wincing when sharp rocks and sticks poked at her feet. He shortened his stride because of her, and she was grateful. Despite how painstakingly slow they were moving, she felt herself growing breathless with exertion.

She was clearly out of shape, because Duncan acted like this was a stroll in the park. She tried to control her breathing so she didn't sound like a wounded grizzly. Between her aching feet and her shortness of breath, she was slowing them down.

What she wouldn't give for a four-wheeler. A minibike. Even a horse. She'd learned to ride when her family had moved to Wyoming, but the hotel kept her too busy to have horses of her own.

She took a step. And another. Winced when she stepped on a rock, then took another.

Chelsey had no idea what time it was. Or how long they'd been climbing. But when Duncan came to an abrupt halt, she plowed into him from behind.

"Oomph." Her face smooshed into his back.

"You okay?" His low voice was barely audible.

"Yes." In contrast to his ability to be quiet, her whisper sounded like a shout.

Duncan turned and gently tugged her down to the ground. She wanted to collapse against him but forced herself to be strong.

"Wait here." He moved away without making a sound. How did he do that?

Suddenly it occurred to her that she was

holding him back. That if not for his willingness to protect her, he'd be long gone and safe.

Instead he'd fought an assailant for her. Led her through the darkness and put her needs before his. Caring for her in a way no one ever had.

In the months since her mother's death, she hadn't felt very close to God. Hadn't been able to feel His presence, even at church. Brett hadn't been much of a churchgoer, and she'd skipped several Sunday sermons doing things with him.

But now, she knew God was still watching over her, despite how she'd strayed.

Humbled, she closed her eyes and thanked God for bringing Duncan to Jackson, Wyoming, and for providing him the strength and courage he needed to keep her safe.

He stared out into the darkness, surveying the area.

Nope. He didn't like it.

The water source was fine, but they weren't far enough from their previous campsite. In fact, he'd been pretty much following the stream they'd discovered earlier. They needed to keep moving, but he could tell Chelsey was losing strength. Her ragged breathing concerned him. The altitude was getting to her, and they weren't even that far up the slope.

He bent down to drink some water, then realized she was still wearing his jacket so he wasn't able to bring water back to Chelsey using his pockets the way he had before.

Sitting back on his heels, he tried to think of what their best decision would be.

Keep going? Or stay here?

Neither option was very appealing.

He estimated the hour to be roughly two in the morning. It would be reasonable to stay here and rest a bit until dawn. It wasn't as if they could move quickly anyway. In fact, he'd worried that her white dress would be a beacon to any of the other men who may be crawling the mountain looking for them.

Okay, they'd stay. For now. He stood and quickly made his way back to where Chelsey waited.

But he didn't see her. His heart squeezed and he raked his gaze over the area, peering through the darkness. The moonlight offered just enough light that he could see the trees and rocks around him.

"Chelsey." He tried not to let his internal panic show in his voice.

There was nothing but silence for a long moment.

"Here." He caught a glimpse of white as she lifted her arm to wave.

His shoulders slumped in relief. In his absence, she'd covered her white gown in dirt and leaves, doing a good job of blending in with the foliage. She'd obviously learned from him and he had to smile at her ingenuity.

Thankfully she was okay.

He crossed over to take her hand in his,

drawing her upright. It took every ounce of willpower he possessed not to pull her into his arms and hold her close.

No need to let her know how scared he'd been.

"This way." He took her hand and led her over several large rocks to the stream. When she saw the water, she dropped down and leaned over to drink.

"Thank you." Her gratitude made him uncomfortable. So far he hadn't done the best job of protecting her. They should have continued hiking while they'd had light or found a better place to hide for the night. He should have doused the fire.

Maybe if he'd done a better job, the bad guys wouldn't have found them.

"We'll stay here," he said, gesturing to the trio of trees, "until dawn."

"Can you make another fire?" She gamely followed him to the meager shelter.

"No. That's how they found us the first time."

"Okay." She shivered, and even in the darkness he could tell she was apprehensive. "It will be okay. You're going to rest against me, and I'll keep you warm." He sat with his back up against two of the three tree trunks, and gently pulled her down beside him. She stretched out so that she was lying against his chest, his tux jacket pulled up over her back like a blanket. He wrapped his arms around her and hoped she wouldn't become too chilled.

The last thing he needed was for her to get sick.

She relaxed against him, clearly exhausted from their brief hike. He kept his arms around her, hoping she'd absorb some of his warmth.

Sharing their body heat was essential for staying alive, but he couldn't deny that holding Chelsey was nice. He closed his eyes, reminding himself that not only had Chelsey just lost her fiancé, but he wasn't in the market for a relationship. Losing the woman he'd loved several years ago to a violent crime was bad enough. Amanda had been brutally attacked and robbed on her way home from work late one night and died from bleeding into her brain. Sitting at her bedside for almost a full week, he couldn't believe it when she was gone. No way was he opening his heart to that kind of pain again.

Besides, his life was back in Milwaukee, Wisconsin, not here in Jackson, Wyoming. Sure, the Grand Teton mountains were incredibly beautiful, but his dad, his sister, his nephew, his niece and friends were all back home.

Everyone important in his life.

Although, that wasn't exactly true any longer. Seeing Chelsey again made him realize how much he cared about her.

But only as a friend. He couldn't afford to lose another piece of himself the way he had after Amanda had died.

FOUR

Chelsey huddled against Duncan, his tux tucked over her shoulder, reveling in his warmth and strength despite the eerie darkness surrounding them.

How was it possible that she felt so safe in his arms?

She closed her eyes and tried to sleep, knowing rest would be critical to her ability to hike out of there in the morning. But the rush of adrenaline, the aftermath of their close call, raced through her veins. Her mind kept going back to those terrifying moments when she thought they both might die at the hands of the assailant.

"Chelsey, please try to relax." His deep voice rumbled in his chest beneath her ear. "Morning will be here soon and we'll need to be ready to move."

"Okay. Are you going to try to sleep, too?" she whispered.

"Yes." His simple answer surprised her. "But not until you do, because your tenseness is keeping me awake."

A reluctant smile tugged at the corner of her mouth. It never failed to amaze her how in tune he was to her emotions. Or maybe it was just being in danger that was bringing them so close together. She drew a deep breath in, then let it out, trying to relax the tension from her muscles.

"Much better," he murmured. "Sleep now, Chelsey. You're safe with me."

"I know." She took another deep breath and felt a strange calmness settle over her. Maybe because she knew she was safe with Duncan.

And more so because she was certain God was watching over them.

She must have dozed at some point, because she awoke with a start.

"Shh," Duncan whispered.

She froze, her heart thumping wildly against her chest. The sounds of the forest should have been reassuring, but she couldn't be certain what had awoken her.

"A buck, see?" Duncan lifted his hand, pointing in the direction off to their right.

At first she didn't see anything, then heard the sharp snap of a twig. She realized it was the same sound that had brought her awake.

A dark shadow moved and the light of the moon fell across the deer's golden coat. He was an impressive animal with a large rack of antlers stretching up to the sky over his head. The animal sniffed the air for a moment, and she wondered if he'd smelled them because he abruptly turned and headed down the mountain.

"Beautiful," she whispered.

She felt him give a soft kiss to the top of her head. "Yes," Duncan agreed.

A blush crept up her cheeks and she was glad it was still dark. She shifted slightly, hoping she wasn't squashing him too badly. "What time is it?"

"About four thirty in the morning," Duncan said softly. She really needed to figure out how he spoke so quietly. "In another hour, we'll need to move."

An hour. She closed her eyes and tried to fall back asleep. It was no use.

Fifteen minutes later, Duncan led her back to the stream so they could drink again. It may have been her imagination, but she thought the area looked a little brighter. Dawn rose early, because the mountains didn't block the sunrise from the east.

"Let me check your feet," Duncan said when she finished drinking from the stream.

She pulled up the edge of her wedding dress, revealing her tattered ballet slippers barely held together by the strips they'd wrapped around them.

Duncan frowned with concern. "We need more strips from your gown."

"Hiking boots would work, too," she quipped trying to lighten things up.

He didn't smile. "Maybe I should try to have you hide somewhere until I can get help."

She reached out and grabbed his hand, her chest squeezing with fear. "Please don't leave me, Duncan. I'll be fine."

Duncan didn't look convinced. He pulled out the larger knife he'd taken from the assailant and went to work cutting away more of her gown. When he was finished, he wrapped the strips around her feet and up her calves, then back down again in a way that reminded her of the old gladiators. It seemed to work—the fabric added good support.

"Thank you."

Duncan rocked back on his heels for a moment, regarding her thoughtfully. He looked as if he wanted to say something, but then slowly stood and offered his hand. She took it, allowing him to help her to her feet.

Once again, he led the way through the forest, taking some sort of route that only a mouse would call a trail. She pushed the bobby pins back in her hair to keep the curls from falling into her eyes and concentrated on keeping pace with him, stepping where he did to avoid rocks and sticks.

Moving quietly seemed an impossible task and she had no idea how Duncan was managing it. Even when she followed in his exact footsteps, she made more noise than he did.

Was he right about other assailants being out there? Were they combing the side of the mountain, looking for them?

Lord, please keep us safe in Your care, amen.

The sun rose as they walked, brightening the area around them. Time had no meaning—without a watch or a phone she didn't have a good way to know how long they'd been on the move.

But it felt like forever.

Duncan slowed and lifted a hand in warning. She froze, straining to listen. After a moment he turned toward her. "Need a break?"

"Yes."

He nodded and gestured to the left. "There's an outcropping of rock that way. Follow me."

She nodded. After all, she'd been following him since this mess started, which seemed like a long time ago, but was really just over fourteen hours.

A lifetime.

They reached the rock slab five minutes later. She leaned against it for a moment, trailing her gaze over the area. It almost looked like a spot where someone would hike to in order to get a nice view. Even though they were tucked beneath the overhang, she could tell the rock was high enough that one might be able to see the entire valley below.

"We've come farther than I thought," she said in amazement.

Duncan nodded. He pulled out his cell phone and lifted it up. "I've got one bar, but my battery is less than fifteen percent."

She tried not to show her disappointment. "Probably because I used the flashlight app."

"You saved our lives, no need to apologize for that." Duncan punched in a number on the phone and listened. After a long moment, he grimaced. "Nothing. Even with one bar, I can't get through."

She shivered, realizing they were really on their own. She looked out over the landscape again, her gaze stumbling over what appeared to be a square corner.

A structure? She stared hard, trying to make it out. As dawn brightened, the corner became clearer and more evident. "Duncan, is that a cabin?"

His gaze sharpened. "Where?"

She lifted her hand, pointing toward the bit of brown that could be seen through the trees. "See the two pine trees that are taller than the others?"

"Yes." He narrowed his gaze. "I see it now. You're right, I think it's a cabin. The square angle isn't natural, but appears man-made."

"I say we head in that direction." Chelsey couldn't hide her excitement. "Maybe there will be something in there we can use, or food to eat."

"Maybe." Duncan's voice held a note of caution. "It's a good idea to check it out."

"Lead the way," she said, feeling giddy with relief. A cabin meant a roof over their heads if nothing else.

Unless it was occupied.

No, she refused to go there. The cabin would be empty and provide them something to eat.

She refused to consider any other options.

Duncan had to give Chelsey credit for finding the cabin. Her eagle eye had caught something he'd missed. At the same time, he hoped she didn't have high expectations of what they might find inside.

The place could be something that had been abandoned years ago, falling apart without anything useful left behind. Food and clothing would be great, but he was prepared for the worst. He was hungry, his stomach rumbling loud enough to be heard by the bad guys following them, and he knew Chelsey was hungry, too.

The cabin or whatever structure they found would be better than nothing, at least providing enough protection that they could start a small fire without being noticed. Food would come next. With the gun and knife he'd taken from the assailant, he had a decent chance of successfully hunting something for them to eat.

He headed out through the dense foliage, keeping his pace slow enough for Chelsey to follow him. The best thing about the cabin was that she might be able to remain safe there for a while. He was very concerned about her feet—any cut she sustained might become infected and that would hamper their ability to keep moving out of harm's way.

He'd carry her if needed; it wouldn't be the first time as he'd carried fellow soldiers far heavier than Chelsey out of Afghanistan. Yet moving quietly through the brush with her over his shoulders would be extremely difficult.

Duncan told himself not to borrow trouble, they were doing okay so far. The cabin looked to be roughly a hundred yards away drawing a straight line, which wasn't at all how they'd be traveling.

Chelsey sucked in a harsh breath. He turned to look at her. "You okay?"

She grimaced and nodded. "Found another rock, that's all."

He hesitated, wondering if he should carry her now before she seriously injured herself. He judged the condition of the path between them and the cabin and decided they could keep walking.

Ducking beneath a low hanging branch, he heard another muffled groan at the exact same time a shot rang out. He twisted and threw himself over Chelsey.

"Are you hurt?" he asked anxiously. In his mind the gunfire had come after her groan, but he couldn't be certain.

"Other than you being on top of me?" she whispered. "I'm fine."

He eased his weight to the side so he wasn't squashing her. Relief that she hadn't been hit by a bullet made him a little light-headed, but he shook it off. "Come on, we need more cover."

"Okay."

He moved backward along the ground with agonizing slowness, hoping and praying Chelsey would be able to follow without giving away their location.

The bullet had come from a distance, likely the shooter using a rifle with a scope. Any rustling of leaves could potentially draw another shot.

They weren't far from the base of a tree. With infinite sloth-like movements, he made his way to the tree, using the trunk as meager cover.

Chelsey joined him a minute later, and he was impressed by how well she'd been able to follow his example, slithering along the ground.

When he had her tucked behind his body, he found a rock, lifted it up and tossed it off in the direction from where they had been, watching as it ruffled the leaves on the trees before hitting the ground with a thud.

Instantly the crack of a rifle echoed around them.

Duncan blew out a breath. Okay, then. There was obviously a sniper out there, watching the area for any sign of them.

"What are we going to do?" Chelsey asked in a hoarse whisper.

It was a very good question, and he desperately needed to formulate a plan. The gun he'd taken off the assailant was of little use against a sniper sitting off in the distance using a high-powered rifle.

He stretched out his arm, snagged another rock and tossed it off in the opposite direction from where he'd thrown the first one. Again, another gunshot rang out.

Leaning over, he pressed his mouth near Chelsey's ear. "I'm going to continue drawing their fire while you make your way to the cabin."

"Me?" Her voice was laced with panic. "Alone?"

"Yes." He glanced around their hiding area, wondering how many more rocks and pinecones he'd need to use so that she could get safely to the cabin.

To what he hoped and prayed was a cabin. And not a figment of their imagination.

"I can't leave you here alone. I think we need to stick together."

Normally he'd agree with her, but not

under these circumstances. "Chelsey, you can't stay here. Eventually they'll figure out where we're located." He paused long enough to toss a pinecone. The resulting crack of the rifle came like clockwork, as if the sniper had every intention of sitting there and firing no matter how much ammunition he used.

Which meant the shooter had a significant amount on his person.

No rationing needed.

Chelsey picked up a rock and threw it, but it didn't go very far. Another gunshot rang out, and Duncan put a hand on her head, keeping her down.

"The best way you can help me is to get to the cabin." He couldn't hide the pleading in his tone. "For me, Chelsey. You have to do this for me."

"I'm scared," she whispered.

"I know, but I'll keep diverting their attention until you're safe."

"And then you'll meet me there?"

"Yes." He met her gaze with his. "I need

you to trust me on this. Once you're at the cabin, I can move quicker without worrying about your ability to follow me."

A long minute passed before she reluctantly nodded. "Okay, I'll do it."

"Thank you." He couldn't hide his relief. "Here's how we're going to do this. The second I throw the rock, you're going to move, but stay on your belly, crawling like we did in order to get here, okay?"

She drew in a deep breath and nodded. "Yes."

"Each time I throw something, they're going to shoot. That's your cue to keep moving."

"Got it."

He hesitated, then added, "I want you to take my phone."

Her gaze clouded with worry. "Why?"

"Just in case." He didn't want to worry her, but there was the slim possibility that they might eventually start shooting within the diameter of the moving trees.

It was what he'd do, if he was the one sitting in a tree with a rifle and a scope.

"In case what?" Her blue eyes were wide with apprehension.

He smiled reassuringly. "In case there's better reception up there. You might be able to call the police to help get us out of this mess."

"Oh, okay." She relaxed. "That's a good idea."

He didn't really think the police would be able to help them, but he would do anything to get Chelsey out of harm's way. "Ready?"

She nodded and pushed up off the ground to her hands and knees.

When he lifted his arm to throw a rock, she began to crawl away in the general direction of the cabin. The rock landed and the gunshot immediately followed.

He glanced back in time to see Chelsey disappear beneath the brush.

Good. He let out a long breath and began reaching for more rocks and pinecones.

It wouldn't be easy for Chelsey to cover a hundred yards crawling on her hands and knees. But he was determined to give her every opportunity to get to safety.

Even if that meant sacrificing himself.

FIVE

Chelsey flinched at every gunshot but didn't let fear stop her. She continued to make progress. If she thought walking in makeshift shoes was difficult, crawling along the ground with her dress hiked up over her knees was far worse.

She ignored the pain in her hands, elbows and knees fully aware that Duncan was doing this for her. He'd given her his phone and was doing everything possible to protect her. It was only right that she did her fair share.

Crawl, pause, crawl, pause, crawl. In her mind, she found herself praying with each stretch of crawling.

Keep us safe, Lord, she chanted over and over again, seeking solace.

Glancing behind her, she tried to gauge how far she'd gone. There was no sign of Duncan, but that didn't mean much. He was no doubt hiding in the brush.

She continued making her way in the general direction of the cabin, hoping and praying the place would offer better shelter.

Her dress snagged on just about everything around her. Bugs flew into her mouth, making her grimace, but she kept on moving. The dress and the bugs didn't matter, survival did. And she told herself it could be worse. Rain or snow would make it impossible to crawl to safety.

The minutes stretched into ten, then twenty. She found herself wondering if she'd gotten off course. When she came upon a large tree, she slowly stood leaning on the tree and hiding herself as much as possible to check her progress.

She had veered a little off course, but not bad. The corner of the cabin was easier to see now. It was a brown wooden building with a black shingled roof. The structure looked to be in decent shape and a surge of excitement hit hard.

It was so close!

Staying upright, she made her way toward the cabin using trees and shrubs as cover. It was amazing how much faster she could go now that she was walking. Duncan's phone was tucked into the bodice of her gown and she couldn't wait to reach the cabin to see if she could pick up a signal.

As she reached the cabin, she slowed and strained to listen. She didn't want to barge in on someone. Easing closer, she edged up to a window. A thick layer of dust made it difficult to see through, but the lower portion of the window was broken, so she peered inside.

The place appeared deserted. There were a few bare bones items of furniture, a rough table in the kitchen and a moldy-looking sofa. There may have been something in the bedroom, but she couldn't tell from this angle.

Moving away from the window, she moved around to the front door. It hung off-kilter from disuse. As she stood there uncertainly, it occurred to her that she hadn't heard a gunshot recently. Because Duncan was on his way? She hoped and prayed that was the case. After shooting a fugitive glance over her shoulder, she pushed at the door.

It didn't budge.

No! She tried again, using all of her strength against the warped door.

It opened, not a lot, but about a foot. Enough of an opening for her to slip through.

The interior was darker than she'd have liked thanks to the thick layer of dust covering the windows. The place smelled musty, and up close she could see that the sofa had been ravaged by mice and other small animals.

She moved gingerly through the small

space. There was a kitchen and living area, with a single bedroom and what was once a bathroom. Her initial excitement at having an actual bathroom evaporated when she saw there was no water in the black toilet.

Yuck. She returned to the kitchen area, opening cupboards to see if there was anything to eat.

Her heart thumped wildly when she found a couple of cans of soup and beef stew. Gingerly picking up the cans, she looked for an expiration date.

They were good for another month. Next she searched for pots and pans, but found only a rusty frying pan.

Her hope deflated. Cans without something to cook the contents weren't very helpful.

Moving toward the broken window, she looked outside. Still no gunfire. Was that good or bad? They hadn't found Duncan and hurt him, had they?

She pulled his phone out and held it

up, squinting in the dim light to see how many bars he had. Only one. She dialed 911 and listened.

Nothing. No ringing, no one answering on the other end.

Drawing a deep breath, she lowered the phone. Turning away from the window, she swept her gaze over the cabin. How long had it been abandoned? No way was anyone living here under these conditions.

The doorway to the bedroom hung ajar. The interior was darker than the rest of the cabin and she wondered why. As she moved toward it, she heard the sound of a twig snapping.

She froze, then hurried inside the bedroom. Something dark covered the windows, and the musty smell was even stronger in here. She wrinkled her nose, fighting the urge to sneeze.

"Chelsey?"

Duncan's voice nearly had her weeping in relief. "In here!" She rushed out of the bedroom and threw herself into his arms.

He clutched her close, wrapping his strong arms around her as if sensing her fear. "Shh, it's okay. We're safe."

"I'm so glad you're here." Her voice was muffled against his shirt.

"You did great, Chelsey. But we can't stay long," he warned. "Did you find anything useful?"

She lifted her head and forced herself to step out of his arms. She gathered herself and nodded. "Two cans of soup and two cans of beef stew but nothing to cook them in. Oh, and no cell phone service here, either. I tried." She offered him the phone back.

"Clothes?" he asked, setting the phone aside.

She glanced back at the bedroom. "I'll look, but it smells really musty in there."

"Better musty than visible from a hundred yards away." Duncan smiled and slipped past her. She followed, wondering if they'd find anything useful.

Duncan ripped aside the brown drapes

over the window so they could see better. There was a quilt on the bed that may have been a bit moth-eaten, but he tugged it off the bed and handed it to her. "Be careful, but I need you to go outside and shake this out. We can use it for warmth."

"Okay." Beggars couldn't be choosers, right? She eased out the door, staying well hidden behind the tress, and shook the quilt trying not to imagine bed bugs or other creepy crawlies falling to the ground.

When she was satisfied, she crept back inside to find Duncan standing near the kitchen table. "Look what I found." He held up an army-green boxy thing.

"What is it?"

"A canteen. We'll be able to carry water with us as we hike."

It didn't look like a canteen, not that she was an expert on camping equipment.

"I also found a couple of T-shirts, jeans, socks and one pair of hiking shoes." He displayed them proudly as if they were better than gold, which was true. "The shoes are for you. I know they'll be too big, but probably safer than the ballet slippers that are falling apart."

She eyed them warily. "The clothes will be too big, too."

"We'll make a belt from what's left of your dress." He gestured at her filthy, torn and tattered gown that she still wore.

"Okay, I'll see what I can do." She swept the shoes, socks, shirt and jeans into her arms and returned to the bedroom.

She had to admit that getting out of the dress made her feel light and free. It had been weighing her down more than she'd realized. Not just the fabric itself, but the entire incident.

The wedding that shouldn't have happened. The groom that should have been safe but was now dead.

Tossing the dress aside, she thought of Brett. Her good friend who had supported her in the aftermath of losing her mother. He'd been so sweet and so kind.

And all she'd done was gotten him killed.

Well, not her personally, but the situation.

She closed her eyes for a moment and sent up a silent apology to him.

I'm so sorry, Brett. Please forgive me.

The tightness eased and she picked up the T-shirt and slipped it over her head. It was large, hanging down to midthigh, but not bad. She removed the ballet slippers, the fabric falling away as the seams finally gave up the fight. Resigned, she pulled the socks on next, which were also large, and then the jeans.

The denim was stiff and scratchy, and the waistband gaped at her waist by a good couple of inches. She took a moment to search the room for a belt, but didn't find one. Sitting on the edge of the bed, she pulled on the hiking boots, which were also too big.

Glancing at the remains of the ballet slippers, she decided that hiking boots that were too big had to be better than nothing which was her only alternative at the moment.

"You decent?" Duncan asked from the main room.

"Yes." She stood and held the jeans in place with one hand. "I'll need you to help me make a belt."

"Happy to do that." He entered the bedroom, wearing borrowed clothes as well that fit him far better than hers. The only difference was that he still wore his rented dress shoes so that she could have the hiking boots. He grinned. "You look great."

"Wow, thanks." She shook her head wryly. "Who would have thought wearing borrowed and wrong-sized clothing would feel so good?"

"We'll be able to move through the woods easier now, which is exactly what we need." After making her a belt from her wedding dress, he then balled up some extra fabric and knelt at her feet. He unlaced the hiking boot, then stuffed the fabric into the wide toe area. He glanced up at her. "Place your foot in and see what you think. Hopefully this will prevent your feet from sliding around too much."

"It feels much better than what I had before," she admitted.

He repeated the process with the other boot, then rose to his feet and offered his hand. "Ready?"

She placed her hand in his, took a deep breath and nodded. "Ready."

He gently squeezed her fingers and drew her from the bedroom. On the table he had the canteen and the canned goods, along with a sack fashioned out of his filthy dress shirt.

Duncan slung the makeshift pack over his shoulder then tucked the moth-eaten quilt under his arm, before heading to the door, clearly expecting her to follow.

She hesitated, glancing once more around the cabin.

Leaving the shelter they'd found was more difficult than she'd imagined.

But she forced herself to move, putting her faith and trust in Duncan.

And in God.

Duncan hesitated in the narrow opening of the doorway, searching for any sign of danger. He had no idea if the gunman had gotten a glimpse of Chelsey as she'd made her way toward the cabin or not.

The last two rocks he'd thrown had not drawn gunfire. The lack of response confirmed his fear that the shooter was onto him. He'd moved swiftly after that, blending into the foliage with skills he'd learned in Afghanistan eating up the distance to the cabin in order to catch up with Chelsey.

As much as he'd hoped to stay at the cabin, starting a fire and maybe spending the night, there was no way to do that now. Not when he knew full well danger was lurking out there, waiting for them.

Seeing nothing out of place, he eased

outside. Chelsey was behind him, and he reached out to take her hand in his.

They could move easier now, and he wanted to get as far from the cabin as possible. If the shooter had a scope and managed to see the cabin, he'd know to head over and look for them there.

Duncan wanted to be long gone before anyone arrived.

"Where are we going?" Chelsey asked, as he melted into the forest.

"Mostly due east." He kept his voice low. "I think there's a small town at the base of the mountain in that direction. If we can find the trail it should take us directly there. Brett mentioned hiking it once."

She nodded. "The town of Moose is at the base of Moose Mountain. But it's very small, not a lot of people."

He shrugged and kept moving. "I don't need a lot of people, just a way to reach the authorities."

"Sounds good." Chelsey fell silent, although he was glad she was able to keep up with him as they made their way through the woods. He wanted time to stop and eat, but needed to be sure they were safe first.

They hiked for nearly an hour before Duncan gave her the sign to stop. He'd filled the canteen at a nearby spring, offering it to Chelsey first.

She took a swig, then tried to hand it back. He gestured for her to drink more. "We have to keep hydrated, remember? And there are many streams around here."

After a moment's hesitation, she took another, longer drink. He took the canteen and helped himself, then glanced around.

"I think we should take a quick break and eat the beef stew."

Hope flared in her eyes. "Are you sure?"

"Yes." His military training had taught him to survive on less, but it had been several years since he'd gone without rations for twenty-four hours. He could push on, but that wasn't fair to Chelsey.

She needed to keep her strength up. And food was critical to that goal.

He knelt on the ground and opened the makeshift pack. The cans of soup would be good, too, but salty without the ability to water them down a bit.

"Are we eating it cold?" Chelsey asked, sitting on the ground next to him.

"Yes." Using the knife he'd taken from the assailant, he opened the cans of beef stew and offered one to Chelsey. They didn't have utensils, so he handed her his penknife, choosing to use the large sharp knife for himself.

Even cold, the beef stew tasted good, satisfying the rumbling in his stomach. Glancing at Chelsey, he took note of how she'd eaten hers with gusto, too.

"Never thought a can of cold beef stew could be so delicious," she said with a wry smile.

He let out a low chuckle. "Agreed."

"Now what?"

"I'm sorry, but we have to keep moving." He placed the empty cans and the canteen back in the makeshift pack. "It's best if we make the most of the daylight."

"It seems like we've been walking for hours, but I understand. We should wash the wound on your arm first, though, while we have fresh water." She pushed to her feet with a determined look on her face.

He reluctantly nodded. "Okay."

Her gaze was earnest as she washed the nearly three-inch laceration on his arm. "I wish we had bandages," she muttered.

"Soon," he promised.

"Okay." She stepped back and pushed her hair out of her eyes. "Let's do this."

He estimated the time was just after nine in the morning, so she was right about how it felt as if they'd been walking for hours.

They had been. But they were making good time now which gave him hope. As much as he didn't want to use the normal trails, he felt they needed to get back to civilization as soon as possible.

The bad guys were still out there, and he wasn't sure how many of them there were. The guy who'd attacked him, and the sniper for sure.

How many others? He had no idea.

As he picked up the pace he wondered whether or not the local authorities were out searching for him and Chelsey yet. After all, they'd taken off from the scene of a crime. His first instinct had been to keep Chelsey out of harm's way, but now they needed help from the local police, or park rangers.

Any law enforcement agency would do.

He pulled his cell phone out and held it up again. The screen was completely blank. He pressed the power button to be sure, but still nothing.

Dead as a doorknob.

He tucked it away and continued searching for the trail he desperately hoped wasn't too far off. Although what he knew about the Grand Tetons would fill a postcard.

A rustling noise made him stop dead, holding up a hand to warn Chelsey not to say anything. A tall man wearing a cowboy hat, of all things, emerged from the brush to his right, as if he'd come up alongside them.

Duncan reached for the gun, but the man held up his weapon and pointed at the star pinned to his shirt. "Don't. I'm Slade Brooks from the US Marshals Service."

With one hand, Duncan tried to tuck Chelsey behind him as he eyed the stranger. The silver star on his chest looked real, but that didn't necessarily mean he was one of the good guys.

"How did you find us?" Duncan asked, trying to come up with an escape plan. This guy stumbling across them was too much of a coincidence.

"I've been looking for you both since you took off after Brett Thompson was shot and killed." The marshal didn't move.

"I picked up your trail early this morning, following bits of fabric from Ms. Robards's wedding dress."

Duncan narrowed his gaze. "If that's true, why wait until now to come out of hiding?"

"I wasn't exactly right behind you," Brooks said. "Tracking is one of my areas of expertise, but when I heard the gunshots, I was forced to hunker down and stay low. Fortunately, I managed to find the cabin, saw the discarded wedding dress and realized you were there. Now I finally caught up to you."

Duncan hesitated, unsure if he should buy this guy's story. "Why are the marshals involved?"

Brooks glanced at Chelsey. "Because we know Ms. Robards is in danger. I'm Brett Thompson's handler—he was joining the witness protection program as soon as the wedding was over."

"Witness protection?" Chelsey echoed, pulling away from him so that she could face the marshal. "Why would Brett do that?"

"Because he was going to testify against the owner of the Coyote Creek Construction company." Slade Brooks frowned. "We had a job lined up for him as a security guard in Florida, along with new names and identities for the two of you. You're saying you didn't know anything about it?"

"No!" All the color faded from Chelsey's cheeks to the point Duncan feared she'd pass out. He reached out and placed a reassuring hand on her arm.

Brett's strange story about a new job made sense in a way, but still, Duncan couldn't believe his old friend had planned to do all of this without telling Chelsey. Or him.

Obviously, Brett's delay in going into WITSEC had resulted in his murder.

SIX

Witness protection.

The phrase echoed over and over in Chelsey's mind, yet she was still having trouble comprehending what she'd been told by the US marshal.

Brett had witnessed a crime? And had been about to go into witness protection, taking her with him? Without saying a word ahead of time? Marrying her without indicating they'd be forced to move, to relocate to Florida of all places under a different name and identity?

A flash of anger hit hard. How dare he? How could Brett even consider doing something like that? Marry her, then turn her entire world upside down? As if the danger alone wasn't bad enough, she didn't like Florida. It was far too hot in the summer.

Her knees felt weak and she did her best to lock them in place, remaining upright with an effort. Wordlessly, Duncan slid his arm around her waist and drew her close, offering his support.

Gratefully, she leaned against him, her mind still reeling. As upset as she was with Brett, she was forced to accept that in reality, this was more her fault than his.

Because she'd agreed to marry him, despite not being in love with him. Why hadn't she called off the wedding before it came to this?

If she'd looked deep into her heart earlier, maybe she'd have understood her feelings weren't love as much as friendship. Needing someone, anyone to be with after losing her mother.

There was no denying that if she'd handled this differently, Brett would still be alive.

And she wouldn't be in danger.

"We need to go." The marshal's low drawl interrupted her thoughts. "Ms. Robards's safety is our main concern."

"I...just can't believe this." She drew in a deep breath, then sternly told herself to get over it. There was no way to go back and change the past. Besides, the US marshal was right—they couldn't stand here on the mountain sheltered by the trees indefinitely.

They had to get to civilization, the sooner the better. "Okay, I'm ready."

Duncan gently hugged her, then loosened his grip. "We need to keep Chelsey between us since she's the one in danger."

"Agreed," the marshal said.

"I was planning to head into Moose," Duncan said to the marshal. "But if you have a better idea, Marshal Brooks, I'm willing to adapt."

"Moose works, and you may as well call me Slade," he said and she heard a hint of Texas in his voice. "Easier all around."

Duncan nodded. "I'm Duncan O'Hare,

a cop with the Milwaukee Police Department."

"I know," Slade responded. "We dug into your background when you arrived to stand up as Brett's best man." He turned toward Chelsey. "Stay behind me, Ms. Robards."

"Chelsey," she corrected, falling in step as directed. Duncan covered her back and as they continued on their way, she hoped and prayed he wouldn't get hurt.

Brett had done a disservice to Duncan, too. Inviting him to come to Wyoming to stand up in the wedding, knowing he was in danger.

Not that there was anything she could do about that now. If not for Duncan, she'd be dead.

The tip of her oversize hiking boot caught a tree root, sending her stumbling into Slade. "Sorry," she muttered.

"It's no problem," he drawled. "I'm glad you found something to wear other than the dress."

"Me, too." She wasn't going to point out that her feet were still moving around inside the hiking boots, causing blisters to form. There wasn't anything the US marshal or Duncan could do to change it.

All she could do was to pray they'd reach the town of Moose soon.

"Chelsey, let us know when you need a break," Duncan said. "We can rest as needed."

"Okay." Truthfully she preferred to keep going, mostly because there was no way of knowing if the gunman was following them the way Slade had.

It had never occurred to her that bits of fabric from her dress may have left a trail. Slade had said that tracking was his area of expertise, but what if the gunman or the assailant had the same sort of skill?

She glanced fearfully over her shoulder. Duncan lifted a brow. "You okay?"

"Yes." She continued walking, choosing the placement of her feet very carefully, doing her best to mimic what Slade was doing.

Being sandwiched between the two men was reassuring. She knew in her heart they would both protect her—in a way Brett had not.

She gave herself a mental shake. Brett was gone, and blaming him, sullying his memory wasn't the answer.

But as they continued moving through the forest, she found herself wondering what would happen when they reached Moose.

She wanted nothing more than for her life to get back to normal. To return to the Teton Valley Hotel she owned and managed. Who was taking care of things in her absence? Hopefully Trish was handling everything okay.

Yet somehow, she didn't think that was going to happen. In fact, she had a very sick feeling that her life wouldn't be going back to normal anytime soon.

Maybe never.

* * *

Duncan's emotions swung between relief and suspicion related to the timing of Slade's finding them on the mountain. Granted, the guy seemed to be legit, and he could see how they may have left enough of a trail to follow considering the condition of Chelsey's wedding dress. But he also knew getting a marshal badge wasn't impossible and a variety of scenarios filtered through his mind.

Slade could be taking them straight into the hands of the men who'd murdered Brett, turning him and Chelsey over for a wad of cash. Or Slade could be taking them on a route leading them deeper into the woods, rather than heading to Moose, Wyoming.

He mentally kicked himself for offering Moose as an option. Too late now, but he wished he'd have made Slade come up with the plan.

The marshal had allowed him to keep his weapon, which was a point in his favor. But Duncan wasn't about to relax his guard around the so-called marshal. If his sister, Shayla, was here, she'd tell him to place his fears and worries in God's hands.

Too bad he wasn't sure how to do that. And even if he could learn to pray, better that his focus be centered on protecting Chelsey.

Slade paused, glancing down at what appeared to be a compass in his hand. At least the guy had come prepared. Duncan turned and swept his gaze over the wooded area, checking for anything amiss.

A flock of birds abruptly shot out of a tree as if startled by something. "Get down," he hissed, tugging on Chelsey's bulky jeans. She dropped beside him. Slade went down, too, but pulled his weapon, holding it at the ready.

For long moments there was nothing but silence.

"What happened?" Slade asked in a low voice.

"Something startled those birds from the tree located to the left of center behind us. Could be our sniper is setting up another spot from which to shoot."

"This way," Slade urged, gesturing toward a dense bush near the base of a large oak.

Chelsey's blue eyes were wide with fear as Duncan gestured for her to follow Slade. When he was certain they were both well hidden, he crawled after them, using all the skills he'd learned in Afghanistan to cover his tracks.

Chelsey reached out to grasp his arm when he crept up to her. "Duncan, how long do we have to stay here?"

He glanced over her shoulder at Slade, who looked grim. If the guy was working with the assailants, he deserved an award for his acting skills. Some of the tension in his chest eased with the thought that two people protecting Chelsey was far better than one. "I don't know. If I had proper camouflage clothing, I could double back, find him and take him out of the picture once and for all."

Chelsey's grip tightened. "No! I don't want you to leave."

Her concern for his well-being was touching, and he felt there was an excess of admiration in her eyes, probably because of the way they'd been forced to rely on each other to get through this. He wanted to reassure her but didn't have the words.

And he didn't want to lie, either. Even if Slade was legit, they were far from getting out of this mess.

"I have to agree. I'd rather you stick here with us," Slade whispered. "I can call for reinforcements from the Marshals Service, but that will take time we don't currently have."

"Does your phone work up here?" Duncan asked. "Mine is dead, but even before the battery gave out, I had no service."

Slade pulled out his phone, stared at the screen then frowned. "Nope. But maybe service will pick up once we get closer to Moose."

"Maybe." Duncan wasn't convinced. He glanced around, trying to come up with a plan. They were hidden from the area where the birds had flown out of the tree, but still in the open more than he'd have liked.

Reaching for his knife, he began to cut parts of brush from their hiding place. As if understanding his plan, Slade joined him.

"What are you doing?" Confusion colored Chelsey's gaze. "Starting a fire?"

"No, we're going to use this to help hide us from view." Duncan took a clump of brush and stuck it down the back of her T-shirt. "Like this, see?"

"What good will this do?"

Chelsey's whisper held a note of disbelief.

"It will help us blend into the foliage,

so that we are less of a target," Slade explained.

Duncan nodded, eyeing the marshal with reluctant approval. "Yes."

The process took longer than he'd have liked but soon the three of them were covered in leaves and twigs to the best of their ability. Chelsey had even woven them into her hair, securing them in place with pins without complaint.

They continued on their path toward Moose, Wyoming. Slade remained in front, Chelsey in the middle and Duncan covering her six. They went much slower now, moving from one tree to the next without making too many jarring moves.

The woods behind them remained eerily silent. Duncan briefly considered that the birds leaving the tree so abruptly was a fluke, scared off by an animal instead of a human, but he wasn't willing to take the chance.

Not with Chelsey's life.

He hadn't been with Amanda when

she'd needed him. Thankfully, he was able to be here for Chelsey now. After an hour, Slade lifted his hand, indicating it was time to take a break. They sat beneath the base of a tree.

"I have protein bars for you." Slade pulled them from a small pack.

"We have water." Duncan offered the canteen.

"And two cans of soup," Chelsey chimed in. "Nothing to use as a pan, or a fire to use as a heat source."

"We'll save the soup in case we need to shelter in the woods overnight," Slade said, handing out the protein bars.

"Overnight?" Chelsey looked horrified, the protein bar in her hand temporarily forgotten. "Won't we reach Moose by nightfall?"

Slade looked to Duncan for help.

"May I borrow your compass?" Duncan asked him.

"Sure." The marshal handed it over.

He held up the compass, verifying their

course. He pictured the map in his head, the one he and Brett had reviewed as they were discussing hiking trails. From what he could tell, they were headed in the correct direction, but how far had they come?

He had no idea.

"We'll do our best, Chelsey," he whispered. "But you need to know there is a possibility we won't make it to Moose before dark."

She lowered her chin, staring down at the ground for several seconds before nodding. "Okay."

He longed to pull her into his arms, to tell her everything would be all right and he'd always keep her safe. But it wasn't his nature to make promises he couldn't keep.

Especially to Chelsey, who deserved so much better.

The leaves pinned in her hair itched, the branches stuck into her T-shirt scraped against her skin. She hadn't thought things could get worse, but at the moment it was all Chelsey could do not to break down and cry.

Stupid problems, really, compared to being safe. But she felt as if bugs and spiders were crawling around on her skin beneath her clothes and she absolutely hated creepy crawlies.

It was all so overwhelming. They went from being in danger to being safe, then more danger, until she began to wonder if she'd ever, in this lifetime, feel safe again.

She took a bite of the protein bar, reveling in the taste. The cold beef stew they'd eaten was hours ago, and her stomach had been rumbling for the past ninety minutes. Likely loud enough for Slade to hear, which is why he'd taken a break.

She hated feeling as if she was slowing them down. Her feet were beginning to burn with blisters, and she couldn't wait to get someplace to shower, change and tend to her aches and pains.

Which reminded her of Duncan's injury. She turned toward him. "How's your arm?"

"Fine." He didn't even look down at it.

Slade frowned. "I have a first aid kit."

Duncan shrugged. "No point in fixing it up now, while we're still hiking through the woods. I'll clean it up again when we reach Moose."

When we reach Moose. Not if. Chelsey held on to that thought as they once again trekked down the mountain.

Their progress was slow. Slade abruptly stopped, lifting his hand, cautioning them to be silent. She held her breath, but then he turned to look at her and Duncan.

"We're close," he said. His green eyes were bright with excitement. "I think Moose is only about a mile from here."

"How do you know?" Chelsey whispered. She could see only trees. Endless trees.

"Listen," Slade urged.

She listened, but still didn't hear anything. But then she heard it, the faint echo of music. Country and western music.

"I'm glad Moose isn't far, but we still need to be careful in case the sniper is tracking us," Duncan cautioned.

"Yep." Slade grinned. "At least we won't have to spend the night on the mountain."

"Roger that," Duncan muttered.

Chelsey wholeheartedly agreed. To know the end of this unnerving hike was so close filled her with eager anticipation. This time, when Slade gave the signal to continue moving down the trail, she found it easy to ignore the blisters on her feet, to forget about the leaves and twigs sticking all over her body, itching like mad.

Even a town as small as Moose must have a motel room with a bed, right? And real food? They wouldn't need to eat cold soup out of cans or more protein bars.

What she wouldn't give for a thick, juicy steak.

She concentrated on the soft echo of music, using it as a beacon calling them to safety. The music grew slightly louder, and she found herself silently singing along with the old country and western song.

Slade must have felt they were out of danger, because he picked up the pace. It wasn't easy for her to follow, the overly large hiking boots clumsy and awkward.

"Easy, Slade," Duncan called. "We can't run down the mountain."

The marshal shot a guilty look over his shoulder. "Sorry. I just want to get Chelsey to safety."

"We both do," Duncan said.

"All of us need to be safe," she corrected. "I'm sure by now Duncan is a target, too. Especially after the way he took care of the assailant."

"What assailant?" Slade asked with a scowl. "You didn't mention that earlier."

"I'll explain later," Duncan advised.

The woods around them thinned as they grew closer to the base of the mountain. Chelsey felt almost light-headed with relief.

They were going to make it.

Without warning, the crack of a gun-shot rang out, followed by a second one. Chelsey froze, but Duncan yanked her down to the ground beside him.

Slade had whirled around and dropped to his knees while drawing his weapon, his gaze raking the area.

"I knew there was a sniper back there," Duncan whispered harshly.

"Anyone hurt?" Slade asked.

Chelsey looked down at herself, taking in the baggy jeans cinched around her waist and the long T-shirt. No blood, thankfully. "I'm okay," she managed.

"Me, too." Duncan's expression was grim. "Lead the way to shelter, Slade."

"But aren't we heading down toward Moose? It's not that far," Chelsey protested.

"Not yet," Duncan said. "Not while this guy has a scope trained on us."

She stared at him in horror. "You mean we have to wait him out?"

Duncan grimaced. "I'm afraid so. We should be able to move once it's dark."

Dark? She swallowed a cry and turned to look in the direction the music was coming from. From here, she could just make out a scattering of buildings, still too far to see details, but enough to know they'd be safe.

A wave of despair hit hard. Moose, Wyoming, was so close, yet so far away.

SEVEN

Duncan had suspected the shooter, if there was one, would wait until they had cleared the forest to take his shot.

He hated being proven right.

Fear and disappointment radiated off Chelsey in waves. He glanced at Slade, who wore a grim expression.

"Darkness is still at least three hours away." Slade pulled out his phone and held it up. "I have two bars and can call for reinforcements."

"Like who?" Duncan asked. "Does Moose have any sort of law enforcement?"

"Many park services employees live there," Slade responded. "For all we know they're heading this way now after hearing the gunfire. June is not exactly hunting season."

Chelsey perked up at that comment. "We'll be rescued soon?"

"If I can get through to the park services." Slade lifted his phone and pulled up the number for park services. When he dialed the number, a smile creased his features when the call went through.

"This is US Marshal Slade Brooks requesting backup," he said. "The gunfire you heard was intended for a woman I'm trying to protect."

It went against Duncan's instincts to bring more people into this, but they obviously didn't have a choice.

"We are only about a half mile from the outskirts of Moose, hiding in a thicket of trees. We'd appreciate your assistance." Slade listened, then added, "That would be great, thanks."

"They're coming to get us?" Chelsey asked hopefully.

Slade grinned. "With a four-wheeler."

Duncan nodded his approval. "That's good. Hopefully the shooter will realize that making another attempt at Chelsey with park rangers surrounding her is a bad idea."

"Hasn't stopped them from trying while you and Slade are beside me," she pointed out dryly.

"True, but the shooter doesn't know I'm a cop, and maybe doesn't understand that Slade is a US marshal," he pointed out. In his experience most bad guys didn't make the decision to take out a law enforcement officer lightly.

Yet for all they knew, these guys who'd come for Chelsey couldn't care less as long as they successfully executed their mission. Guns for hire? Maybe.

"I don't hear the music anymore," Chelsey whispered.

"Listen for the sound of a four-wheeler," he suggested.

A hint of a smile tugged at the corner of her mouth. Her face was streaked with dirt, twigs and leaves in her hair, and her clothes, but to his eye, she was still the most beautiful woman in the world.

Strong, too, considering how well she was holding it together despite her entire world being turned upside down.

No point in blaming Brett since their childhood friend had paid for his mistake with his life. All Duncan could do was focus on saving Chelsey.

He wondered if she realized that she would need to go into witness protection to keep safe. He wasn't sure she'd thought that far into the future, but he had.

The thought of never seeing Chelsey again made his chest tight. While it was the right thing to do to keep her safe, he didn't like it.

Not one bit.

Although he wasn't interested in a relationship, he was still her friend.

They sat in silence for several long moments before the sound of a rumbling engine reached their ears. Still, they remained hidden in the brush, waiting for the four-wheeler carrying two park rangers to arrive.

Slade emerged from the brush first. He flashed his credentials. "I'm US Marshal Slade Brooks." He gestured to Duncan and Chelsey. "And this is Chelsey Robards and Duncan O'Hare. Duncan is a police officer with the Milwaukee PD."

"Milwaukee?" One of the park rangers lifted a brow. "You're a long way from Wisconsin."

"Tell me about it," Duncan muttered. He helped Chelsey to her feet. "We appreciate your assistance. I'd like to make sure Chelsey arrives in Moose without being injured."

The park ranger riding shotgun jumped down and crossed over to them. "I'm Ranger Paul Davidson, and the driver is Eric Connolly. We plan to get all of you safely into town."

Duncan, Slade and Paul hovered around Chelsey as they escorted her to the four-wheeler. Duncan helped her inside, then took a seat beside her.

"Keep your head down, Chelsey," he advised. "Bend over, so that you're as small a target as possible."

She did as he requested as Slade climbed in on the other side of her. Paul returned to the front seat of the four-wheeler. The back was crowded, but Duncan didn't care. Between his broad shoulders and Slade's, the shooter wouldn't get a clear shot at Chelsey.

Duncan swept his gaze over the forest as the rangers drove them toward Moose. No gunfire rang out, no sudden rush of wildlife indicating an intruder.

The sniper was either hunkering down until nightfall or was already gone.

Over the roar of the engine, he could hear the sounds of country and western music starting up again. Must be some sort of live band that had just returned from taking a break.

When they'd gotten into the very small,

unincorporated town of Moose, Wyoming, Duncan lightly stroked Chelsey's back. "You can sit up now."

She slowly unfurled herself, looking around at the various small cabins with a look of unfettered relief. "We made it."

"Yeah." Duncan longed to pull her into his arms. "Paul, do you have a motel nearby?"

"Yes, we're taking you there now." The ranger glanced at them over his shoulder. "Looks like you all could use food and clothing, too."

"A shower, clothes including soft shoes that fit and food...in that order," Chelsey said with a sigh.

"Soon," Duncan promised.

The park rangers pulled up to a small, ten-unit motel. Duncan glanced at Slade. "I have cash. It wouldn't be smart to leave a paper trail."

"Agreed, I have cash too, and can get more if needed." Slade waved a hand. "Stay here, I'll get the rooms."

Fifteen minutes later, they were settled in two rooms located right next to each other. Duncan would have preferred connecting rooms, but Moose was too small to offer those accommodations.

"They have a two-bedroom cabin that will be available starting tomorrow," Slade said as he unlocked the door to Chelsey's room. "I've asked them to hold it for us."

"Great." Duncan followed Chelsey into her motel room as Slade moved on to open the next door. It looked like every other hotel room across the country, except maybe for the view of the Grand Tetons. "I'll pick up what you need, just give me a list."

Chelsey blushed and shook her head. "If it's all the same to you, I'd like to pick out what I need."

He hesitated, wishing he could wrap her in bulletproof clothing and keep her hidden from view. But she likely needed personal items, so he gave in. "Okay."

Thankfully, there was a general shop located directly across from the motel. He picked out a few things for himself, then waited for Chelsey to finish before paying for everything in cash.

"I have money at home," Chelsey told him. She clutched the bag of clothing and personal items to her chest as if it were filled with gold.

"Don't worry about it." He didn't have the heart to tell her she wasn't going to be returning home anytime soon.

If ever.

"Do you smell that?" She sniffed the air appreciatively. "Smells like roasted corn and barbequed ribs."

That made him smile. "We'll eat as soon as we clean up." He kept his gaze out for anything suspicious as they crossed the street to the motel.

"I'll be ready in twenty minutes," Chelsey promised as she unlocked her door. "I'm too hungry to wait any longer."

"Sounds good."

He waited until Chelsey closed and

locked her door, before entering his own room. Slade glanced up at him. "Reinforcements should be on their way soon."

"More US marshals?" He dropped his bag of clothes and shoes on the bed closest to the bathroom.

Slade nodded. "A couple of guys I trust with my life, Colt Nelson and Tanner Wilcox."

He forced a nod, inwardly wincing at the idea of more people being brought into this. If he had his way, he'd contact his brother-in-law, Mike Callahan, and the soldiers he'd fought alongside in Afghanistan, Hawk Jacobson and Ryker Tillman, for help. Those were the men he trusted with his life.

And Chelsey's.

But very soon, he wouldn't be in the picture at all. This was a case involving the US marshals and evidence Brett had uncovered while working at Coyote Creek Construction. It was only a matter of time before the US marshals whisked Chelsey away and stashed her someplace safe.

Leaving him behind.

A hot shower with soap and shampoo had never felt so good.

Dressing in plain clothes that actually fit was wonderful. Chelsey never wanted to wear another wedding dress ever again. She placed various Band-Aids on her open blisters, then gingerly drew on cotton socks and slipped her feet into the running shoes she'd gotten from the store. Brushing her damp, curly shoulder-length hair, she used a couple of bobby pins to keep it out of her face, then let it air dry.

Exactly twenty minutes later, there was a light rap on her door. Smoothing the cotton top over the waistband of her jeans, she crossed over and opened it. Duncan, showered and shaved, looked handsome dressed in black jeans and a black T-shirt.

Her heart gave a betraying thump in her chest. She tried to ignore it. This attraction she felt toward Duncan had to stop. She'd mistaken her feelings toward Brett for something more than friendship. No way was she going to make the same mistake again.

"Ready to go?" Duncan held out his hand.

She didn't hesitate to place her palm in his. "Yes." Belatedly she noticed Slade standing behind him. "I'm famished, those protein bars disappeared a long time ago."

Slade smiled wryly. "I'm sure they did."

She clutched Duncan's hand tightly as they walked to the restaurant attached to the motel. Tantalizing scents wafted toward her, making her mouth water. For one brief moment it was as if all the madness of the past forty-eight hours hadn't happened. This could be a nice dinner out with a friend.

Slade's phone rang as they were escorted to a table in the corner of the restaurant. "Colt? What's your ETA?"

Chelsey glanced at Duncan with confusion. He avoided her gaze and pulled out a chair for her, taking a seat beside her.

"What's going on?" she asked in a low voice. "Who's Colt?"

"Another US marshal." Duncan's serious expression gave her a twinge of concern.

Slade disconnected from the call and slid the phone in his pocket beneath the five-point silver star on his chest. "Colt will be here by tomorrow afternoon. Tanner has a conflict. We'll make a game plan once Colt arrives."

"What kind of game plan?" Chelsey glanced between the two men. "Are both Colt and Tanner US marshals?"

"Yes, they are."

She wrinkled her brow. "I still don't understand."

"Can I get you all something to drink?" Their female server was dressed in skintight denim jeans, cowboy boots and a short-sleeved Western-style shirt.

"Actually, I'm ready to order my meal,"

Chelsey said, glancing at the men. "Just water to drink, and I'd love some barbecued ribs and grilled corn, with a side salad, please."

"I'll have the same," Duncan chimed in.

"Make that three," Slade said. "Thanks."

"I'll be back shortly with your water."

"Let's eat first," Duncan said with a pointed look at Slade. "We can talk freely back at the motel."

"Good idea," Slade agreed.

Chelsey felt as if there was something she was missing. When their server returned with a tall glass of water for each of them, she took a long, grateful drink.

Never again would she take food, water and shelter for granted.

"I need a phone so I can call my assistant manager at the hotel," she said to Duncan. "I'm sure Trish is frantic by now."

"Trish—your maid of honor, right?" Duncan asked.

She nodded. "I need to let her know I'm okay, and that I'll be back soon."

There was a long silence as the two men studiously avoided looking at her. A chill rippled down her back. "What? Are you saying I won't be back soon?"

"Chelsey, we need to keep you safe." Duncan's tone was gentle. "Let's just take things one step at a time, okay?"

She didn't like the sound of that.

"Chelsey, I want you to think about what Brett said to you over the past couple of weeks." Slade gazed at her over the rim of his glass. "We can't discuss it here, but think about it. Even the slightest detail might help."

Help what? She wasn't sure.

Their meals arrived a few minutes later, and Chelsey made time to offer a quick prayer to God before diving in. The tangy barbecue sauce was incredible, and she savored every bite.

They finished eating thirty minutes later. Chelsey had saved half her food and insisted on a to-go bag. The men walked on either side of her as they returned to the motel.

After putting her leftovers in the mini fridge in her room, she joined the guys next door. "I'm sorry, but I don't remember Brett talking about anything recently except for the wedding."

Slade pinned her with a narrow look. "Nothing about his work with Coyote Creek Construction?"

She frowned. "The company headquarters are in Cheyenne, but they also have a small branch in Jackson. We planned on adding a wing at the Teton Valley Hotel, using Coyote Creek Construction, but nothing else."

"Nothing about the man he worked for? Anthony Nettles?"

Chelsey slowly shook her head. "Never heard of him. Brett mentioned Kenny Martin—I thought he was the boss."

"He's the general manager working under Anthony Nettles," Slade said. "Have you met Kenny Martin?"

She frowned. "I went to the Jackson office to meet Brett once. He was talking to some guy, and when I asked who he was, Brett said he was Kenny Martin. He was a slender guy, about the same height as Brett, but with thinning dirty blond hair."

Slade let out a heavy sigh. "Brett never mentioned Anthony Nettles, or anything about being in witness protection?"

"Not a word." She pushed aside the useless anger. "Is that why you have more marshals coming? To find out who Brett spoke to? He obviously can't be a witness for you anymore."

There was a long pause.

"Tell her," Duncan said in a curt tone.

"We lost a witness in Brett, that's true. But the problem is that the men who silenced your fiancé are now after you. There's no easy way to say this, Chelsey, but you'll be placed in witness protection as soon as possible. For your own safety."

"I'm—what?" She glanced at Duncan,

then back at Slade. "No, that's not happening."

"Chelsey, please..." Duncan began, but she shot out of her chair.

"No. I can't leave my life behind to become someone else!" She yanked the motel door open and headed to her room. Duncan was hot on her heels, and she abruptly swung around to face him.

"Leave me alone. I can't talk to you right now."

"Chelsey, please. I understand you're upset..."

"Upset?" A harsh laugh erupted from her throat. "You have no idea."

Hot tears sprang to her eyes and she swiped at them impatiently. She should have known this was coming. Should have realized that the gunmen wouldn't rest until she was dead.

Literally or figuratively.

Duncan's arms came around her, pulling her into his warm embrace. She wanted to rant and scream and kick, but found herself melting against him. She took several deep breaths, trying to pull herself together.

"I'm sorry," Duncan whispered.

She shook her head. "It's not your fault."

He continued to hold her, smoothing a hand down her back as if she were a child needing comfort. After what seemed like forever, she lifted her head and looked up at him.

Their gazes locked—the world around them grinding to an abrupt halt.

He gently lowered his head to press a chaste kiss on her cheek. But that wasn't what she wanted. When he lifted his head, she went up on her tiptoes to capture his mouth in a sweet kiss.

This. This was what she'd wanted from the moment Duncan had arrived in Wyoming.

Not to kiss Brett, but Duncan.

EIGHT

Chelsey's kiss caught Duncan off guard, but that didn't stop him from deepening the kiss. A tiny voice in the back of his mind warned him that this wasn't real, that Chelsey's kiss was a reaction to everything she was dealing with, but another part of him didn't care.

He'd liked and admired Chelsey when they were younger, but had kept his feelings firmly in the friendship bucket. Then Brett had announced their engagement, which made her off-limits.

Brett was gone, but Chelsey wasn't ready for this.

And neither was he, although at the moment Amanda's memory was fading fast.

She broke off from their kiss, her breathing just as erratic as his. He tucked her head beneath his chin and simply held her, without saying anything. His heart ached for what she was facing, through no fault of her own.

After several long moments, he asked, "Are you okay?"

She drew in a deep, ragged breath and nodded. She lifted her head to look up at him. "I have to be."

"You have every right to fall apart, Chelsey. We can't be strong all the time."

Her smile was sad. "God will get me through this. I just have to place my faith in Him. And in the US Marshals Service. It's just..." her voice trailed off.

"I know." He understood that giving up the life she'd built wasn't easy. In fact, he thought this would be the most difficult thing she'd face.

Well, other than running away from bad guys with guns.

"Would you like me to stay with you for a while?" He felt helpless, unable to do anything that might ease her distress over giving up everything to enter WITSEC.

"No, I'll be okay." She offered a weary smile. "After all the hiking and lack of sleep over the past few days, I'm looking forward to being in a real bed again."

He forced himself to loosen his grip and step back. "All right, but if anything changes I'm right next door. Don't hesitate to come get me."

"I won't." She watched as he turned toward the door.

He glanced over his shoulder. "Lock up."

She nodded and he stood outside her door, satisfied to hear the click as she shot the dead bolt home.

For a moment he pressed his palm against her door, then chided himself for being foolish. When he entered the room he shared with Slade, he found the guy on the phone again.

"I need a computer, any chance you can get one?"

Duncan listened to the one-sided conversation as a way to distance himself from how he'd been rocked by Chelsey's kiss. Slade's frustration was apparent as he scowled.

"Okay, fine. Tomorrow will have to do." Slade disconnected from the call and scrubbed his hands over his face. "There's a lot to be done, but I don't have the tools I need."

Duncan dropped onto the edge of the bed. "Like what?"

"We had an identity picked out for Brett and Chelsey, but now she needs something entirely new. I can't trust that Brett didn't blab to someone about what was going on."

Duncan nodded slowly, his pulse kicking up at the possibility of having Chelsey nearby for a while longer. "What about the guy Brett was planning to testify against? Shouldn't we continue that investigation as well?"

Slade shot him a glare. "We? There is

no we here, Duncan. I appreciate every-thing you've done, but this is a US Marshals case. A cop from Milwaukee doesn't have any jurisdiction here."

Duncan frowned. "I'm aware of that, but you should use my expertise to your advantage. Brett told me a wild story about being hired on to provide security for a wealthy rancher."

Slade looked interested. "Did he say who?"

"No, and when I mentioned this to Chelsey, she said the only rancher nearby was a guy by the name of Elroy Lansing. Only he's not wealthy at all, has been apparently selling off parcels of land to stay afloat."

"Elroy Lansing," Slade repeated. "That sounds familiar."

"His property is apparently right next to the land owned by Chelsey's hotel."

"But if Lansing doesn't have any money, how could that have anything to do with Brett Thompson?" Slade argued.

"I'm not sure," he admitted. "But Chelsey mentioned Coyote Creek Construction was being hired by the hotel to expand, and their property line meets up with Lansing's." He shrugged. "Maybe it's time to follow the money, see who purchased parcels of land from Lansing in the past year or so. See if there are any ties to Coyote Creek Construction."

"Not a bad idea," Slade said grudgingly. "Once I get my hands on a computer, I'll get on that."

"I can help," Duncan said quietly. He'd borrowed Slade's phone cord to recharge his battery. The two men had exchanged numbers, too. "No reason we can't investigate this thing while we're waiting for everything to be put in place for Chelsey."

Slade didn't comment for a long moment. "You're right. I appreciate having you here, Duncan. I feel better knowing there are two of us keeping her safe."

The tension in Duncan's shoulders eased. "Good." He yawned, exhaustion catching up to him. "Let's discuss strategy in the morning."

Slade nodded and shut off the lights, plunging the room into darkness. Duncan stretched out on the bed fully clothed and closed his eyes.

His last conscious thought was that if they could find the evidence needed to bring the bad guys to justice, it was entirely possible Chelsey wouldn't have to give up her life to enter witness protection.

And he secretly promised to do whatever was necessary to make that happen.

Chelsey awoke at dawn, feeling well rested for the first time in what seemed like forever. At least, until she began to think about the ramifications of giving up her life.

Panic clawed its way up into her throat, robbing her of the ability to breathe. A passage of scripture flashed into her mind from the book of Psalms. *"He shall call upon me, and I will answer him: I will be with him in trouble; I will deliver him, and honour him. With long life will I satisfy him, and shew him my salvation."*

Her emotional turmoil eased and she immediately felt reassured and calm. Leaving Wyoming wouldn't be the worst thing that could happen to her. She would miss her friends; the hotel her parents, grandparents and great-grandparents had worked so hard for; the guests who came to stay on a regular basis.

But she had her faith and her life. Being on the run with Duncan made her realize how grateful she was to be alive.

After a quick shower, she eased open her motel room door, glancing around before heading over to tentatively wake Duncan. He immediately answered her knock, opening the door and gently pulling her inside.

"You look well rested." Duncan's dark gaze didn't miss a thing. "Have a seat. We're ordering breakfast to the room."

"Why?" She took a seat in the only chair.

Duncan shrugged and glanced at Slade. "Just being cautious."

"Okay. I'm just thankful we'll have food to eat," she admitted. "I planned to warm up my leftovers from last night."

"No need for that yet." Duncan squeezed past, the room seemingly small with the two men taking up space. "What would you like?"

"Anything," she said with a smile.

Five minutes later, they'd placed their to-go order. Slade offered to pick it up from the restaurant as the motel was too small to offer room service.

"Check on when we'll have access to the cabin," Duncan suggested.

"Will do." Slade headed for the door. "I'm also going to find out what computer access they might have available. I'll call when I'm on my way back with the food."

The room was silent after Slade left.

Chelsey blushed, remembering the moment she'd kissed Duncan.

And he'd kissed her back.

She cleared her throat. "When are you planning to head back to Wisconsin?"

He looked startled by her question. "Not anytime soon." He paused, then added, "It's possible that if we can find out who killed Brett and arrest the men in charge, you might not need to hide out in witness protection."

A flicker of hope flared in her heart. "Really?"

"I can't say for certain," Duncan hedged. "But it's a possibility. One I can't ignore. I'm hopeful that when Slade gets a computer, we can really dig into the backgrounds of the men involved with Coyote Creek Construction. It's not unheard of for construction companies to have ties to organized crime."

"Organized crime?" Her voice rose with agitation. "I can't believe Brett stumbled across something that caused all of this. And why on earth didn't he confide in me?"

Duncan eyed her steadily for a long moment. "Would you have agreed to marry him if he had?"

"No." The word popped out of her mouth before she could stop it. She grimaced and looked away. "You know I was having doubts anyway. If he had told me anything about witnessing a crime, or entering witness protection I would have ended things long ago."

"We don't know for sure when Brett stumbled across the criminal activity," Duncan said reasonably. "Could be it all happened fast, in the last couple of weeks."

"Maybe. Looking back, it seems like Brett changed about three weeks ago. He became, I don't know, edgy. Impatient but then overly apologetic." She shrugged. "At the time I chalked it all up to prewedding jitters, but now it seems as if that must have been the time this all started."

Three weeks. She couldn't believe Brett had kept all of this a secret for nearly a month.

"We can verify with Slade when he returns with our breakfast." Duncan looked thoughtful. "But one thing that doesn't make a lot of sense to me is why the US Marshals didn't approach you sooner."

A chill snaked down her spine. "You— don't think Slade is faking being a US marshal, do you?"

Duncan blew out a breath. "No, I don't. After all, he helped us escape the mountain by calling the park services. But we need information. He hasn't told us everything he knows. I was so exhausted yesterday, I hadn't really considered the timeline until now."

She sat quietly for a few minutes, trying to think back to those days she'd spent with Brett prior to the wedding. He'd been spending less time in Cheyenne—because he was avoiding the men who he'd witnessed commit a crime? And what exactly had Brett seen?

Duncan was right. They needed answers.

A phone rang. Chelsey instinctively patted her pockets, even though she knew she didn't have a phone. Brides generally didn't have a secret pocket in their wedding dress for a phone.

Although now she wished she'd thought of such a thing.

"Okay, thanks." Duncan disconnected from the call. "Slade is on his way with our food, and we'll be able to move into the cabin rental by ten."

"Is it far from here?" She wasn't sure it was necessary to move into a cabin. The motel rooms worked fine, unless maybe it was cheaper.

"Just a mile or so, and more isolated from the rest of town which is probably a good thing." Duncan rose to his feet and went over to the window overlooking the parking lot. "This feels too close for comfort."

She didn't answer, because she liked being around people. It wouldn't be long before she'd be starting over with a new name and new identity. It wouldn't be the first time she'd had to start over: the move from Milwaukee, Wisconsin, to Jackson, Wyoming, twelve years ago had been a culture shock. The wide-open spaces with the Rocky Mountains in the distance very different than living in the suburbs of Milwaukee.

Where would she end up this time? Hopefully not Florida, she thought with a grimace. California had decent weather, but there were earthquakes to contend with. Maybe back to the Midwest area, Kansas or Nebraska.

None of the options filled her with enthusiasm.

Duncan opened the door for Slade who came in carrying several cardboard containers of food. He handed one to her, then set the others on the desk.

She bowed her head and silently thanked God for providing her food, a bed and support from Duncan and Slade. When she lifted her head, she saw that both Duncan and Slade were waiting for her before eating their meals.

"It's a blessing to be here with you both," she murmured. "I want you to know how grateful I am for everything you've done for me."

Duncan glanced at Slade who looked just as uncomfortable with her expression of gratitude.

"It's my job to keep you safe, Chelsey," Slade said gruffly.

"I feel the same way, Chelsey. You're my friend and I'll do whatever is necessary to keep you from harm," Duncan added.

"Okay, then. Let's eat."

They all dug into their eggs, toast and bacon. Chelsey thought the food tasted amazing—maybe because she now realized the can of cold beef stew had been awful in comparison.

"Did you find a computer?" Duncan asked, glancing at Slade.

The marshal nodded. "I began a quick search on the rancher's property, was able to identify the buyer as a corporation, not a person."

Duncan frowned. "What sort of corporation?"

"Not Coyote Creek Construction," Slade replied dryly. "Something called Elkhorn Estates."

"Elkhorn Estates?" Chelsey looked askance. "Is that some kind of joke?"

"No, that's the listing," Slade replied. "But I have to admit it sounds fake. I didn't have time to dig into it to find the principal owners."

Elkhorn Estates. There were plenty of elk living in the mountains and elk hunting was a big deal in Wyoming. People came from all over the United States to hunt here starting mid-September and going well into November.

But she'd never heard of anything called Elkhorn Estates. "Maybe the plan was to build a subdivision on the land."

"Anything is possible," Slade agreed. "How would that have impacted your hotel business?"

She winced. "Not in a good way, that's for sure. People come to vacation in Jackson, Wyoming, because of the rural setting and the mountains. These are generally people who like to camp, hunt and fish." She waved her plastic fork. "Besides, there aren't enough year-round residents in Jackson to justify a brand new subdivision."

"Unless there was some sort of new business coming into the area to support something like that," Duncan countered. "If a new company opened up shop here, then there would be more employees— some with families, right?"

She nodded slowly. "Yes, but enough to

build a subdivision of homes? That seems like a stretch."

"Do you know how many acres of land Elroy Lansing owned?" Duncan asked.

"At least five hundred, maybe more."

Slade whistled. "That's a lot."

She nodded. "I know it sounds that way, but his father and grandfather before him originally purchased the land for their cattle ranch. From the way Elroy spoke about it, they had well over a thousand head of cattle in their thriving ranch."

"What happened?" Duncan's gaze was curious.

"I wasn't here back then, but according to the rumor mill, Elroy Lansing's father went through a messy divorce, which cost him a lot of cash. He wanted to keep the ranch, so he had to pay his wife for her portion. Then a bunch of the cattle got sick and died."

"Lansing never married?" Slade asked.

"No. Apparently he was in love with a woman who hated the isolation of the ranch. She took off and he decided it was better to remain alone." She finished her breakfast and set the empty cardboard container aside. "What does any of this have to do with Coyote Creek Construction and whatever crime Brett uncovered while working for them?"

"It may not be connected at all," Slade admitted. "I just thought the animal theme was an interesting coincidence."

"This is the Wild West," she pointed out.

"Don't forget Brett told me that he was planning to work security for a wealthy rancher nearby," Duncan said. "It's possible Brett was giving me some sort of clue about what he was involved in. And we don't know how rich or poor Elroy Lansing is. Maybe Elkhorn Estates paid him a pretty penny for his land."

She didn't like hearing the stories Brett had told everyone except her. She turned toward Slade. "What crime exactly did Brett witness anyway? Stolen goods? Drugs?"

The marshal didn't answer for a long moment.

"It has to be something major, or they wouldn't kill him," Duncan added. "And I think Chelsey has a right to know."

Slade slowly nodded. "Okay. Brett witnessed a murder."

Her jaw dropped in shock. "M-murder? Are you sure?"

Slade's expression was grim. "Yes, absolutely. Brett claimed he had proof of the crime and needed a day or two to get it, but we never received anything. We were called in by the local police chief because of the suspected ties to organized crime. They'd had some concerns about Coyote Creek Construction for a while now, and Brett's allegation only added to their belief."

Chelsey felt numb from shock. Murder and organized crime. No wonder Brett had seemed on edge. It hadn't been about prewedding jitters at all.

How horrible to have witnessed a murder.

Yet as bad as she felt for him, the news only proved their relationship wasn't built on trust and love the way she'd thought.

But on secrets and lies.

Depressing, really, to realize she didn't really know anything at all about the man she'd been about to marry. Tears pricked at her eyes at how foolish she'd been.

Tears welled in her eyes. She needed to learn to listen to her gut instincts, which had told her she was making a mistake.

One that had almost gotten her killed.

NINE

"I—I don't understand why Brett wouldn't tell me," Chelsey whispered, swiping at the tears. "He said he loved me. Why would he lie to me if he loved me?"

Duncan had no answer for that. "I'm sorry."

There was a long moment as Slade shifted awkwardly in his seat. "I'm sorry, too. I feel partly responsible for this."

He glanced at Slade. "Yeah, about that. Why didn't you talk to Chelsey about the program?"

Slade winced. "That's a fair question. In my defense, things happened pretty fast. The murder took place just over a week ago, and we were brought in about three days later. I discussed the option of testifying and going into WITSEC with Brett and he agreed to get me the proof he had of the crime, and mentioned the wedding claiming he'd told Chelsey everything. He said he'd promised to give her the wedding she wanted before heading out of town. I had no reason not to believe him."

"But you knew he was in danger," Duncan argued.

"He was off work for the wedding, and to my knowledge no one but those in the Jackson Police Department knew about Brett witnessing a murder and the proof he had of what happened." Slade scowled. "We believed him, but after everything that transpired since, I'm convinced there's a leak within the department."

The spurt of anger faded and Duncan knew this wasn't the time to assign blame. He owned a piece of this mess, himself for not pushing Brett more once he'd realized something was going on. And Brett should have clued in Chelsey, the woman he'd been about to marry.

Now their old childhood friend was dead and there was nothing they could do other than move forward from here. Too bad they didn't have whatever proof Brett thought he could obtain.

"W-who was murdered?" Chelsey asked.

Slade hesitated, shooting a glance at Duncan as if asking for help on how much to say. He nodded, indicating she had a right to know. After all, the shooter already believed she knew. Her trying to play dumb wasn't going to work.

Not at this point. Not when these men had already gone so far as to kill Brett and attempt to kill him and Chelsey, more than once.

"A guy by the name of Roland Perry," Slade said. "He was apparently arguing with his boss. Brett heard the raised voices, and crept closer to see what was going on. According to Brett, his boss, Anthony Nettles, pulled a gun and shot Perry. Brett ducked down, and remained hidden all night, until long after everyone had left. When he came out, he called the police who in turn called us."

A shiver rippled through Chelsey, and he gently squeezed her shoulder reassuringly. "I...see."

"We haven't found the body yet," Slade went on. "And we were waiting for Brett to get us the evidence he'd promised. We did find out that no one has seen or heard from Perry since this took place. Local law enforcement is doing their best to find evidence. Unfortunately, Wyoming has plenty of places to stash a body where the wild animals will find it long before we do."

Chelsey swallowed hard and put a hand over her stomach as if she felt ill. He couldn't blame her. Hearing this made him feel lousy, too.

"It seems as if going back to the local law enforcement isn't an option," Duncan said slowly. "Not if there's a leak."

"Agree." Slade sighed. "I'll feel better

once Colt shows up. For now, our main priority is to keep Chelsey safe."

Duncan nodded, although he wanted to find a way to bring Anthony Nettles to justice so that Chelsey wouldn't have to live out the rest of her life in witness protection.

Maybe Brett had gotten a photo of the argument, or audio taped the shooting. There had to be something that would put Nettles behind bars.

He released Chelsey, and then gathered their garbage together. "Getting her settled in the cabin is a good start."

Slade rose to his feet. "I plan to head over there first, check things out. I can buy supplies, too."

Duncan shot the marshal a glance. "How long do you plan to keep her there?"

"Hopefully not more than twenty-four to forty-eight hours," Slade said. "I'm putting a rush on the new ID and paperwork, but these things take time."

Just two days left to spend with her. His

gut clenched with fear. It wasn't that he didn't trust Slade. The guy's actions so far proved he was legit. But he didn't like the idea of Chelsey going off without him.

After disposing of their garbage, another thought occurred to him. "What about the park rangers?"

Slade lifted a brow. "What about them?"

"Can we trust they won't go to the local law enforcement about the gunfire? And about taking us off the mountain?"

"I made sure they understood this was a federal US Marshals matter, and not one for the locals to get involved in," Slade replied. "They didn't argue and didn't seem concerned about letting me handle things."

Duncan wished he felt reassured. He didn't.

Slade left the motel room, leaving him and Chelsey alone. She stood and reached for the door.

"Wait, where are you going?" He quickly moved beside her.

"My room." She glanced at him. "I don't have much to pack, but would like to take the few things I bought yesterday with me to the cabin."

"That's fine. I'll walk you over." He swept up the key card, and then eased her aside to open the door. Using his body as a shield, he took her arm and escorted her the few steps to her room.

"Thanks." Chelsey's smile didn't reach her eyes. She slipped inside the room and shut the door behind her.

Duncan stood there for a moment, wishing there was something he could do or say to make her feel better.

But there wasn't.

After he returned to his room, he used his phone to call his brother-in-law, Mike Callahan. "Hey, how are Shayla and the kids?"

"Great," Mike replied. "Brodie is being an awesome big brother to his little sister, Breena."

The image of his sister, Mike and their

two kids made him smile. Then his smile faded as he realized he couldn't bring them into this.

He never should have called him.

"Great, glad to hear it." He thought fast. "Listen, I'll be here in Wyoming for a few more days. I'll let our sarge know, but he may need help covering my shifts."

"Yeah, sure. Breena is sleeping like a champ these days, so shouldn't be a problem." Mike paused. "Something wrong?"

"No," he hastened to reassure him. "The Grand Tetons are beautiful. I'm planning to do some hiking while I'm here and wouldn't mind a few days to wind down."

"Alone? Or did you meet up with some pretty cowgirl?" Mike teased. Since all six Callahans were married with kids, they had begun to make it their mission to see him settled as well.

"No cowgirl," he said, despite how the image of Chelsey walking down the aisle in her wedding dress flashed in his mind.

"Just want a few extra days, is all. Thanks Mike, take care of your family."

"Will do. Oh, and by the way, you should be prepared to hear big news from your dad and my mom."

Duncan winced. His dad, Ian O'Hare, was a widower just like Mike's mom, Maggie Callahan. Their respective parents had been spending time together as friends over the past couple of years. Maybe more than friends. As much as he wanted them to be happy, Duncan didn't really want to think too closely about them dating.

Some things were better left unimagined.

"Dunc? Are you there?"

"Yeah." He cleared his throat. "Let me guess, they're getting married."

"I'm getting that vibe, yeah. Just thought you might want to be prepared."

"Thanks for the heads-up, Mike. Listen, I have to call Sarge. See you in a few days." He disconnected from the line before his brother-in-law could say anything more.

His friends, not just the Callahans but Hawk Jacobson and Ryker Tillman were all family men now. They had wives and children of their own. He couldn't bring himself to drag any of them into this.

But he wasn't about to leave Chelsey high and dry, either. He was determined to stay and help protect her.

No matter what.

Hiding in her room was childish, but she needed a few minutes to come to grips with the idea that Brett had witnessed a murder and now those responsible were coming after her.

To kill her.

Retreating to the bathroom, she gathered the few personal items she'd purchased yesterday and placed them in a paper bag provided by the motel for laundry. Just like her hotel did.

She collapsed on the edge of the bed,

feeling numb at the idea of never seeing her family's hotel again. It was only a building, but also a place full of memories.

And all she had left of her parents.

She wondered if Slade and Duncan might be able to get in to get some photographs for her. Tears pricked her eyes again and she swiped at them with annoyance. She wasn't normally a crier, but someone who liked to get things done.

Time to get a grip. There were worse things in the world than not having material items. Or the place your parents lived.

Her life was more important than any of that. She closed her eyes and lifted her heart to God.

Help me, Lord, to understand and accept this new path You've provided for me, amen.

She wasn't sure how long she sat there, but a knock at her door had her rising to her feet. Using the peephole, she saw

Slade standing there. "Hi. The cabin must be ready, huh?"

He nodded. "Yes, it's clean and stocked with food. Stay here, I'll get Duncan."

She stepped back and grabbed her bag. When the men returned, they once again sandwiched her between them as they made their way outside and along the parking lot, keeping parallel to the building.

It felt foolish, and she wondered what the people who lived in Moose, Wyoming, thought about them as they headed toward the rear portion of the motel. In the distance, she could see a cabin, tucked off to the side, isolated from other structures.

Slade held the key in his hand, and Duncan stood guard as the marshal unlocked the door and pushed it open. She crossed the threshold, glancing around curiously. It was nicer than she'd expected, rustic but with a great view of the mountains from the back porch.

"Home, sweet home," she murmured,

dropping her bag of personal items on the glossy oak kitchen table.

"For a couple of days," Slade agreed. He glanced at his watch. "I'm heading back to the motel office to borrow their computer again. Duncan, I'm sure you won't mind staying here to watch over Chelsey."

"I don't mind at all, but I'd like to dig into the Coyote Creek Construction company. Could your marshal friend bring a spare computer? Two brains working on this are better than one."

Slade nodded. "I need to check in with Colt anyway, so I'll see if that's possible."

"What can I do to help?" Chelsey wasn't the type to sit around doing nothing. Managing the hotel had kept her busy, which is what she preferred.

"Honestly, the best thing you can do is try to remember anything Brett may have mentioned about this job at the construction company, the people he worked with, anything at all." Slade smiled. "It's often the littlest things that can break open a case."

"Okay." Slade left and Duncan poked his head into the fridge and the cupboards, scoping out the lunch possibilities even though they'd just finished breakfast.

Taking a seat at the table, she sighed. She didn't hold out much hope of remembering anything helpful. Those past few weeks before the wedding, she'd been dealing with last-minute preparations while studiously ignoring the lingering doubts about her upcoming marriage. Not to mention getting everything in the hotel running smoothly while she was gone on her honeymoon.

She abruptly straightened. Wait a minute, their honeymoon. Brett had done the planning for their trip—all she'd asked for was to be able to swim in the ocean, something she'd never done, and to find a place that wasn't too hot. He'd teased her that he had all her preferences on file, and in fact had carried a file folder with the details.

She remembered he had suggested Florida. Had he settled on it? Maybe the northern part of the state? Was that why Slade had mentioned relocating them there?

"Did you remember something?" Duncan's keen gaze apparently didn't miss a thing.

"Nothing to help with the case, but I just realized Brett did all the planning for our honeymoon, someplace near the ocean because I've never seen it." She stared at him. "Do you think he was waiting until the honeymoon to tell me about being in witness protection? That the place near the ocean was going to be our new home?"

"Maybe." Duncan sat across from her. "Did he say anything else about the trip? Did you have airline tickets or anything?"

"No, although he did have a folder with details that he carried around. What was strange is that he wanted to drive to Florida, so we could see the scenery." She thought back to the snippets of conversation. "He seemed surprised when I mentioned not liking Florida. Do you think he planned to go somewhere else? Like maybe without the help of the US Marshals Service?"

"I hate to say this, but nothing at this point would surprise me. Brett apparently wanted to have a new life with you, no matter what he'd witnessed. Maybe he thought that simply moving away would be enough." Duncan's gaze hardened and she realized he was seriously angry with their friend.

"It's so hard to believe that he would think I would just give up the hotel my family owned to live with him in another state. Doing what? I mean, what was he thinking?" She dropped her gaze to the glossy table. "I don't know what I'm going to do now, when I'm forced to take on a new identity."

He reached out and took her hand. "I know nothing about this is easy, Chelsey, but you're smart and talented. You can do whatever you'd like."

She shook her head. "Not true. I wanted to run the hotel my parents left to me, but that's not possible."

"Try thinking of what you might have done if the hotel had gone under for some reason," he suggested.

"I guess you have a point," she admitted. What would she like to do? She couldn't cook so running a restaurant was out.

But at one time she'd considered becoming a teacher. She had a fine arts degree. Could she put that to use in some way? Maybe.

And what about the so-called proof Brett said he'd get? Duncan's phone rang. He pulled away and stood. "I have to take this, it's my boss."

She listened as Duncan told his boss he needed more time off work. When she realized she was shamelessly eavesdropping, she picked up her bag of personal items and did a quick search of the cabin.

The two bedrooms were on the right side of the house, with a small bathroom between them. She chose the smaller of the two, then set her items in the bathroom. She readjusted the bobby pins in her hair, then moved on.

Catching a glimpse of the Teton mountains out the back window, she moved that way, drawn to the majestic view. That Brett would just relocate her from the mountains because she'd mentioned wanting to swim in the ocean was unfathomable.

A wave of shame hit hard. Living near mountains or the ocean shouldn't be more important than their love for each other. Which was the crux of the matter.

She hadn't loved Brett enough to move anywhere in the world for him.

Which only reminded her of the intensity of Duncan's kiss. Of how much she enjoyed being cradled in his embrace. So different than the sweet fondness she'd felt for Brett.

Kissing Duncan had sparked the old attraction she once had for him. A youthful crush, something she'd grown out of.

Or so she'd thought.

But hadn't she leaned on Brett after losing her mother? Mistaking his kindness and support for something more?

She couldn't make that same mistake with Duncan. He was very attractive, and had saved her life more than once.

It wouldn't be fair to confuse feelings of gratitude toward him for love.

Anxious for some fresh air, she opened the back door and stepped outside, breathing deep. Off in the distance, she could see a bald eagle flying overhead, enjoying the wind off the mountains.

It pained her to give all of this up.

"Chelsey?"

Duncan's voice had her turning to face him. Her feet were still sore, and she missed a step and fell forward at the exact same moment the echo of a gunshot rang out.

"Down! Stay down!" Duncan shouted

as he quickly closed the gap between them. In a swift move he grabbed her arm and hauled her back into the cabin, out of harm's way. When she'd cleared the threshold, he slammed the door shut, then urged her deeper inside the cabin.

"Get under the kitchen table," he said, his voice low and urgent. "Are you okay? Were you hit?"

"I—I don't think so." Her teeth began to chatter. "A-are you sure that was m-meant for me?"

"I'm sure." Duncan's tone was grim. He pulled out his phone. "Slade?" He scowled when he realized he was talking to voice mail. "I need you back here, pronto. Someone just took a shot at Chelsey."

She huddled under the table, realizing at that moment that giving up the mountains would be easy enough as long as it meant staying alive.

TEN

Duncan eased the gun he'd taken off the assailant from his ankle holster and held it ready, sweeping his gaze over the interior of the cabin.

The shot at Chelsey had come from the north, where there was nothing but mountains behind the cabin. The front or south side of the cabin faced the street. It was also the direction they'd come in, less than an hour ago.

How had the sniper known about their relocation?

From the park rangers? Honestly it didn't seem likely. Maybe there was a team of men watching from all sides. The more he thought about that possibility, the more he thought it correct. One shooter couldn't be following them this well. And if they were, why not take a shot while they were outside the motel? Maybe there wasn't a good enough angle from where the sniper was waiting.

Which brought him back to the idea there had to be at least two men involved. And considering the possibility of this being linked to organized crime? Maybe more.

He didn't like it. He lifted his phone to call Slade for the second time, but the marshal's number was already flashing on his screen.

"What happened?" Slade demanded.

"Chelsey stepped out the back door and someone took a shot at her." Duncan kept his voice low, just in case someone was outside close enough to overhear. "Thankfully, they missed, but it's clear they have eyes on the cabin. You need to be careful."

"On my way." Slade disconnected from the call.

Duncan hoped Slade's position as a US

marshal would keep him from becoming a target. He glanced over at Chelsey. "You're sure you're not hurt?"

She nodded and offered a wan smile. "Guess it's a good thing I'm clumsy and tripped over my own feet."

He frowned. "You're not clumsy, but I'm sure your feet are probably still sore from all that hiking."

"A little." She downplayed the injury he felt certain was worse than she was letting on. Despite not having any medic training, he mentally kicked himself for not insisting on checking her feet for injuries. He didn't want her to end up with a raging infection. The wound on his arm had been cleaned out, too, and so far seemed to be okay.

"Slade's on his way back." He stayed crouched beside her, knowing they needed to find a new place for Chelsey soon.

Ten minutes later, Slade rapped on the door and called, "It's me," before using his key to enter the cabin. Duncan slowly rose to his feet when Slade ducked inside, closed and locked the door behind him.

"We need a new location," Duncan said grimly.

Slade sighed. "If I had one, we'd move. There isn't another option at the moment."

"We can't keep her here," he argued. "What's to stop them from peppering the place with bullets?"

"The possibility of getting caught." Slade raked his hand through his hair. "Look, I know staying put isn't optimal, but Moose isn't exactly a large metropolis. The motel and a couple of cabins are all they have to offer. Until we get a set of wheels and reinforcements from the US Marshals Service, we're stuck. And don't forget, there are plenty of armed park service rangers around."

"Wait, you said cabins, plural?" Duncan asked. "Can we swap with someone?"

"And put that person, or worse, an entire family, in danger?" Chelsey crawled out from beneath the table and stood beside him. "No. I'm not doing that."

Okay, she had a point. He turned and glanced around the cabin. "We can stay away from the windows, but I'd feel better if we could cover them with plywood."

Slade nodded. "That's a good idea. I'll check with the park service, see what they might be able to dig up for us. I'm sure they won't mind helping out."

It wasn't much, but he'd take it. He pulled out a kitchen chair for Chelsey. "Please sit down. We'll do our best to make this place safe."

"I guess I shouldn't have gone outside," she murmured with a sigh. "And it's better being stuck in here, then out on the side of the mountain without a place to stay."

"I'm glad you're focusing on the bright side." Duncan took a moment to prioritize which windows needed to be covered. Those in the main cabin, including the large picture window overlooking the mountains, and the ones in Chelsey's bedroom. He glanced at Slade. "We'll need to take turns keeping watch if we have to stay the night."

"Of course." Slade didn't argue. He pulled out his phone. "Give me a minute to contact the park rangers about plywood."

Duncan sat beside Chelsey, thinking back to what she'd said about their honeymoon. "You mentioned Brett had a folder related to your honeymoon. You never saw what was inside?"

She slowly shook her head. "No, he wanted it to be a surprise." Her expression turned resigned. "Apparently a really big surprise, like hey, just so you know I witnessed a murder and we're now going into witness protection."

He felt bad, but dwelling on Brett's lies wasn't going to help. "Think for a moment, Chelsey. If he carried that folder around with him, you must have glimpsed something. Like papers with writing on them? Or maybe pictures of the place you were going to be staying? Anything at all that you can remember?"

"Pictures," she said without hesitation. "I remember they were large and glossy, but I only saw the edges, not the entire photographs."

A buzz of adrenaline shot through him. "Photographs on heavy-duty paper? Or something he printed off the internet?"

"Yes, glossy like heavy-duty paper. Why does it matter?"

Duncan hesitated, wondering if he should confide in her. She must have noticed because she bristled.

"Don't lie to me, Duncan. Not the way Brett did. Not about something as serious as this."

"Okay, I won't lie to you, Chelsey. Not now, not ever." He took a deep breath. "I'm having doubts about Brett. He lied to you, and to me, who's to say he didn't lie to the US Marshals, too? And the local law enforcement?"

She paled. "What kind of lies? You think

he made up the story about witnessing a murder?"

"No—after all, he was murdered for a reason. But what about the part of his story where he claimed to need time to get the evidence? That doesn't ring true to me."

"I see what you mean," she admitted with a frown. "Yet it seems unbelievable that he would actually have evidence but not turn it over to the authorities right away."

"Yeah. Just as irrational as marrying you without saying anything about going into witness protection," he countered dryly. "It makes me wonder if Brett was trying to play this thing from both ends."

"Both ends?" Chelsey's voice was faint. "You mean, he told the bad guys he knew something about them as blackmail?"

"Hang on, Chels, I never said he was blackmailing anyone," he hastened to re-assure her. "I'm sorry if I wasn't clear while I think out loud. Frankly, if Brett had done that, the bad guys would have taken him alive to find out where he hid the evidence." The more he thought it through, the more he didn't believe that Brett would be that reckless. "But I do wonder if he thought he should keep the evidence hidden from the local authorities."

She stared at him as realization dawned. "Because he didn't trust them?"

"Maybe." Or because he wanted something to hold over their heads? He wasn't sure what to think. "Any idea where Brett may have stashed the folder?"

"Most likely my office."

"Your office?" That surprised him.

"Yes, my office. That's where I kept all the other wedding plan files. It didn't matter to me. I was too busy to peek at his honeymoon arrangements," she said defensively.

"Okay, just checking." Duncan glanced up as Slade walked over to join them. "We need to get into the Teton Valley Hotel to search Chelsey's office."

"For what?" Slade frowned.

"A file folder containing photographs that Brett carried around with him. I think there's a possibility that Brett may have taken a picture of the murder."

Slade's green eyes widened. "He did mention needing time to get the evidence to us, but you think he had it all along?"

"Yeah, I do." Duncan was just as frustrated with Brett's actions as anyone. "But I'm starting to wonder if Brett knew more than he let on."

"You really think he kept the evidence at the hotel?" Slade sounded skeptical.

"If Brett didn't tell anyone about the evidence, including law enforcement and any potential leak there, then why not? Why not practically hide it in plain sight? It's possible no one would consider Brett had photographs stashed in Chelsey's office."

"Okay, maybe," Slade said, nodding slowly. "When Colt gets here, we'll discuss this more. For now, the park rangers have agreed to help us out by delivering plywood within the hour."

Duncan would be glad to have the plywood in place, but at the moment he would have rather had a set of wheels.

His instincts were screaming at him that Brett had in fact hidden evidence of the crime he'd witnessed. If not photographs, maybe something else. An audiotape would be nice. Anything pointing to Nettles being a killer.

If they could arrest the guy for murder, there was a chance that Chelsey wouldn't have to go into witness protection.

And despite his determination to keep his heart isolated from being hurt a second time, he was forced to admit he liked the idea of having Chelsey nearby.

Very much.

Chelsey put a hand up to her temple, reassured to find she wasn't bleeding. Horrified to realize the bullet had come so close she'd felt the heat of it zipping past her skin.

She took a moment to thank God for yet again keeping her safe. It seemed the Lord was working overtime with her.

And she appreciated His grace and protection.

Along with Duncan. She glanced at him, his handsome features already imprinted in her mind. He'd reacted instantly to the sound of gunfire, charging toward her, putting himself in danger once again to rescue her.

Duncan was a man of honor. A man of his word. She trusted him in a way she wasn't sure she'd ever trust another man.

She tore her gaze away and tried to focus on the present. The idea of doing something to escape this mess was appealing.

Sitting around doing nothing while waiting for the next bullet to hit its mark wasn't productive. She wanted to do her part in finding the man who'd murdered Brett.

In her mind's eye, she cast her memory back to the last time she'd seen Brett with the honeymoon folder. It had been a yellow folder, because yellow was her favorite color. She'd been charmed by his choice at the time. Now she was just annoyed.

He'd use a yellow file folder because it was her favorite color, but not tell her he'd witnessed a murder that was likely linked to organized crime. Yeah, how was that for twisted?

She tried to shake off the bits of anger that kept floating to the surface. Brett was dead. He'd paid the ultimate price for his mistakes.

Time to get over it, already.

Chelsey closed her eyes and tried to bring the memory into focus. She'd been in her office, finishing up a call with the florist when Brett had ducked his head in, his smile dazzling. He'd had the yellow file folder in his hand, tapping it idly against the door frame as he waited for her to finish.

"Everything okay, Chelsey?"

"It will be. The florist doesn't have enough yellow roses so I'll have to have white intermixed with the yellow. No big deal, though. What's up?"

"Just wanted to say I love you." Brett's smile faded when his cell phone rang. *"Do you mind if I take this quick?"*

"Sure." He came farther into her office, slid the yellow folder on the edge of her desk beneath several other file folders as he stepped away to take the call.

"Yeah, I know he's been AWOL for a while, but I'm sure he'll turn up, he always does." There was a pause before Brett said, *"Of course, I can take over his projects but not until after my wedding and honeymoon. You know how it is, gotta keep the wife happy."*

"Chelsey?" Duncan's tone pulled her from her thoughts. The way he was looking at her made her realize she must have been ignoring him for a while.

"Yes?"

"You okay?" Duncan's tone was full of concern.

"Yes, why?"

"You were staring off into space, frowning." Duncan put his hand on her shoulder and she couldn't stop herself from reaching up to cover it with hers. The warmth from his palm seemed to radiate down to her bones. "Bad memory?"

It was disconcerting the way he read her so well. "Not bad, necessarily, but I just remembered a call Brett took while we were in my office. He had the honeymoon folder with him, and he tucked it beneath a bunch of my files before moving away to take the call."

"You think it's still on your desk?"

She shrugged. "I don't see why it wouldn't be. It was the day before the wedding and we were heading out soon for the rehearsal dinner? But that's not all,

Brett made a comment about a guy being AWOL."

"AWOL is a military term for absent without leave," Duncan said thoughtfully.

"Yes, then he said something like, of course he'd be happy to take over the guy's projects, but not until after the wedding and honeymoon." She didn't add the part about keeping his wife happy, because really it only showed just how clueless Brett was about her feelings. How happy would she have been after the wedding? Not very. She focused on the tidbit of information she'd overheard. "Do you think the guy that went AWOL is the same man who was murdered?"

"It's possible Brett was referring to Roland Perry," Duncan admitted. "The name doesn't ring a bell?"

She slowly shook her head. "No. I remember Brett talking about Kenny Martin, and frankly I assumed that was who he spoke to that day he mentioned the guy going AWOL. But nothing about a Roland Perry."

Duncan gave her shoulder a little squeeze. "Keep up the good work, Chelsey. You've remembered the yellow folder, seeing photographs in there, and this latest conversation Brett had about someone going missing. I'm sure there are other fleeting memories that you've picked up along the way."

"Yeah. Too bad I don't have one of those eidetic memories," she said with a sigh. "That would come in handy right now."

"Good news, I just heard from my buddy Colt Nelson. He'll be here in about an hour with more supplies, like a computer and weapons, along with a nice SUV with tinted windows," Slade informed them.

"I'm glad to hear it," Duncan said, releasing her shoulder to turn toward Slade. "I'd like better odds than what we've been dealing with so far."

Chelsey frowned. "We already have the two of you against the shooter."

Duncan rubbed the back of his neck in a way that told her he had bad news. Before she could remind him of his promise not to lie to her, he said, "I think there's at least two men out there watching us, maybe three."

"Three?" Her pulse jumped and she tried to remain calm.

"Two for sure," Duncan said firmly. "The shooter was stationed to watch the back door, maybe waiting for us to let our guard down long enough to go outside. If he's up in a tree on the mountain, how did he see us come inside through the front door? There has to be someone out front and another guy out back, at a minimum."

Slade nodded, making her realize she was the last to know. She cleared her throat. "Once Colt gets here, will we head to the Teton Valley Hotel?"

The two men exchanged a look. "Maybe later," Duncan reluctantly said. "Once darkness has fallen."

"Jackson isn't that far. We could be there and back in an hour," she pointed out.

"I know," Slade said. "Don't worry, we'll keep you well guarded while we check things out."

"Well guarded?" She glanced between the two men. "I'm coming with you."

Duncan rubbed the back of his neck again. "Chelsey, I know you want to help, but…"

"No, you don't understand. It's not just getting the file folder. I'd also like at least one picture of my parents along with the birthstone pendant they gave me." When she saw the expression in Slade's eyes, she insisted, "Two small things. One picture and a pendant. That can't be too much to ask."

Neither man spoke for a long moment. Finally, Slade sighed and turned to face her.

"I'm sorry, Chelsey, we can let you come along if you insist, but the recommendation from the US marshals is that you take absolutely no personal items with you at all. Not a photograph or a pendant. Anything material that might connect you with your old life is far too much of a risk."

She felt as if she'd been sucker punched in the stomach. No picture of her parents? No birthstone pendant? She put a hand up to her neck, feeling for something that wasn't there. Why hadn't she worn the pendant with her wedding dress? Why had she decided at the last minute to take it off? Because the pendant didn't sit well with her neckline?

So stupid to care about something like that. She lowered her chin to her chest, struggling with the need to cry.

She'd known going into witness protection would be difficult, but until that moment the magnitude of what she was giving up forever hit hard.

And heaven help her, she wasn't sure she could do it.

ELEVEN

Chelsey's grief-stricken expression tugged at his heart. Duncan wished there was something more he could do for her.

Other than finding the evidence that might just put Anthony Nettles in prison for the rest of his life.

A knock on their cabin door had him spinning around, weapon ready. Slade lifted a hand. "Probably the plywood."

Duncan nodded, but didn't necessarily lower his weapon. Survival instincts had been drilled into him during his time in Afghanistan. He wasn't going to relax his guard.

He stood in front of Chelsey as Slade went to the door. To his credit, the marshal called out first. "Who's there?"

"Ranger Eric Connolly. I have the plywood you requested."

Slade eased the door open, verifying the park ranger's identity before allowing him in. Eric entered the cabin, carrying a sheet of plywood, with a tool belt slung over his shoulder.

"I have a small circular saw, hammer and nails," Eric said. "Will two sheets of plywood be enough?"

"I think we can make it work," Slade said. "Thanks, I know this is above and beyond the scope of your duty."

"I don't mind. Want help?" Eric stood for a moment with his hands on his hips, surveying the room. "Shouldn't take long."

"That would be great." Slade and Duncan moved forward, quickly measuring and sawing wood.

The work was mindless, and Duncan couldn't help glancing at his watch, hoping Colt Nelson would get there soon. He wanted some time with the computer, to investigate just who they were dealing with, before heading out to the Teton Valley Hotel to search for Brett's honeymoon folder.

The interior of the cabin turned dark once they had successfully covered the windows. They had just enough plywood for the main living space, and since they'd be heading out that night, decided the bedrooms would remain off-limits for now.

Thirty minutes after Eric left, a black SUV with tinted windows pulled up. Duncan hung back as Slade gestured to his fellow marshal to come inside.

Colt was tall and lean. He had short blond hair beneath the rim of a cowboy hat similar to Slade's which made Duncan wonder if the hat was part of the US marshal uniform, like the five-point silver star on his chest. Colt carried a computer bag over his shoulder, but there was only one device, not two.

"Colt, this is Duncan O'Hare. He's a cop with the Milwaukee Police Department and this is Chelsey Robards," Slade said by way of introduction.

Colt nodded. "I'm Colt with the US Marshals Service. I see you have the place locked up tight."

"There was another attempt to kill Chelsey from someone hiding in the trees behind the cabin," Duncan said.

Colt scowled. "Not good."

"We'll fill you in. Let's unpack your computer and get to work," Duncan suggested.

Slade updated Colt on the recent events as Duncan took charge of the computer. The cabin came with internet access, but it was slow. Still, he managed to come up with a picture of Anthony Nettles, turning the screen so Chelsey could see.

"Recognize him?"

She shook her head. "No, sorry."

"No need to apologize, just trying to work through the list." Duncan went back to work, finally finding a grainy picture of Kenny Martin. "How about this one?"

"Kenny Martin." There was no hesitation in her tone.

Slade leaned over his shoulder. "I remember him. He was at the wedding."

"He was?" Duncan glanced back at the photo. "I guess it's reasonable Brett would invite his boss."

"Unless he knew the guy was mixed up with organized crime," Slade pointed out dryly.

There was that. Brett had obviously not been thinking too clearly about all of this.

"He spent a lot of time talking to someone," Slade continued, staring at the picture on the screen. "An older guy, face like leather, wearing chaps which stuck out to me as it was, after all, a wedding."

"Chaps?" Chelsey echoed. "The only person that wears chaps everywhere is my neighbor Elroy Lansing."

"The rich rancher?" Duncan asked, committing the photograph of Kenny Martin to memory.

"Not rich," Chelsey reminded him.

"He's been selling off his land, remember? Which is why it was always a little sad that he wore chaps, like he was living back in the days when he was herding cattle by horseback."

"Hmm." Duncan wished he'd paid more attention to the guests at Brett and Chelsey's wedding. But they were strangers to him, and he hadn't anticipated Brett being gunned down at the altar.

"Yeah, Brett mentioned Elroy Lansing," Slade said. "We need to look into who owns Elkhorn Estates, the company which bought up a big chunk of Lansing's property."

"That might be outside my area of expertise," Duncan admitted. "I'll give you the computer in a moment." He tried searching for Roland Perry, but nothing came up. After a few minutes of trying, he reluctantly turned the screen toward Slade and gave up his seat. "I give up on Roland Perry. Have at it."

Slade worked the computer like a pro,

despite the frustratingly spotty Wi-Fi. "Whoever owns Elkhorn Estates has covered their tracks really well. The president is listed as Simon Graves." He glanced at Chelsey. "Does that name sound familiar?"

"No," Chelsey said.

"Did you know everyone who was on the guest list for your wedding?" Duncan asked. "Did Brett invite a lot of people?"

Chelsey frowned. "Actually, he didn't. I remember urging him to invite more friends and family, but he kept saying that his aunts, uncles and cousins were too far away and wouldn't want to make the trip to Wyoming."

"Work friends?" Duncan persisted. "He clearly had Kenny Martin on the list."

She looked thoughtful for a moment. "For sure Anthony Nettles wasn't on the list, and neither was Roland Perry. But there were a couple of others. I can't remember their names offhand."

Duncan tried not to show his disappointment. "It's okay, maybe something will come to you."

Colt prowled the interior of the cabin, seemingly antsy to be stuck inside without any natural light. Duncan could relate. After all, he was used to being active, too.

"I'll throw together something for lunch." Chelsey poked her head into the fridge then looked through the cupboards. "Looks like grilled ham and cheese sandwiches are a good choice."

"Fine with me," Slade said absently. His gaze was rooted on the computer screen. "Guys, check this out."

Duncan and Colt hovered around Slade. "Who is that next to Nettles?" Duncan asked.

"According to the local newspaper, he's multimillionaire Travis Wolfe. Almost makes you wonder if good ole Travis isn't the brains behind Elkhorn Estates."

"Chelsey?" Duncan called. When she glanced at him, he gestured for her to come over. "Do you recognize this guy?"

She came over to peer at the photograph. "Yes, I've seen him before."

"When?" Duncan asked.

"I think he and Elroy Lansing were having dinner in our restaurant recently. I remember because their tab was well over $250 for two people and our server was gushing over the generous tip."

"That gives some credence to the possibility that Wolfe is the brains behind Elkhorn Estates," Slade said.

"But how is that connected to Coyote Creek Construction?" Chelsey asked.

"Maybe Coyote Creek Construction was going to be awarded a very lucrative contract to perform all the building associated with the new homes located within Elkhorn Estates?" Duncan offered. He pinned Slade and Colt with his gaze. "Are we sure this is all related to organized crime? Could be just plain and simple greed."

Slade hesitated and shrugged. "It was the locals who insisted they were looking at a potential organized crime ring.

Otherwise why bother to get the feds involved at all?"

It was a good point and one Duncan wasn't sure how to answer.

They already suspected that someone within the Jackson Police Department was leaking information, so why would they want to involve the feds?

It was a mystery for sure, and one that he was beginning to doubt they'd ever solve.

Chelsey was glad to be able to contribute something to the investigation. As she made lunch for the group, she tried to remember if she'd noticed anyone else meeting over dinner at the hotel restaurant.

The faces were all a blur.

How many other deals had been struck under her clueless nose?

"Something smells good, Chelsey," Slade said with a smile. He was a nice guy, jet black hair cut short beneath his cowboy hat, which he'd taken off while inside.

"Almost ready," she promised.

Colt's hair was as light as Slade's was dark. Colt was slender and tall while Slade was broader across the shoulders. The two men seemed intent on seeing to her safety, and as much as she appreciated their efforts, she wished she could go back to her life as she knew it.

Which was a useless thought.

When two grilled ham and cheese sandwiches were ready, she slid them onto a plate and set it in the center of the table, then prepared to make more.

By the time they'd all finished eating the hour was early afternoon. She was in the process of cleaning the kitchen when a shrieking alarm went off with enough force to pierce eardrums.

"What is that?" she asked, trying to be heard above the noise.

"Car alarm." Colt pulled his weapon and opened the front door of the cabin just enough to see outside. "It's equipped to go off when anyone touches the vehicle."

Chelsey frowned. That seemed a little overkill considering anyone could brush up against a car.

"Let's check it out," Slade said, joining Colt at the door. The two men eased outside.

Duncan locked the door behind them, then crossed over to stand beside her. They didn't try to talk—it was impossible to carry on a conversation over the screaming alarm.

The sound stopped as abruptly as it started. Chelsey let out a breath she hadn't realized she'd been holding and rubbed her ears. "That hurt."

"Yeah." Duncan's expression was serious. "But it's nice to have."

"I would think it gives off false alarms more often than helping," she argued. "I mean, come on, who's to say a dog didn't run past the vehicle and thump it with his tail?"

"And who's to say it wasn't someone with malicious intent?" Duncan retorted. "I'd rather have a half-dozen false alarms if it scares away one bad guy."

Maybe he was right. This wasn't the world she normally lived in. Worrying about bad guys and hiding from murderers had never so much as blipped on her radar screen.

Until now.

After what seemed like forever, the two US marshals came back inside the cabin, twin grim expressions marring their features.

Colt held up a small circular device. "Someone tried to put a tracker on the SUV."

A tracker? She stared at the thing in horror.

"We need to get out of here." Duncan's tone held a hint of anger.

"We agreed to wait until dark," Slade countered. "And waiting will only make it more difficult to track us by sight."

"I've reengaged the car alarm," Colt added. "They won't make the mistake of trying to put a GPS device on again."

"I don't like it, Slade. We're sitting ducks here, and they know it." Tension radiated off Duncan. She placed a reassuring hand on his arm.

"We're also in the middle of nowhere, Wyoming." Slade spread his hands. "There isn't a lot of traffic out here. We could be easily tailed back to Jackson."

"They may guess we're heading there anyway," Colt said. "I mean, there's only so many places to go on this side of the state. If we were closer to one of the bigger cites, like Laramie or Cheyenne, it would be easier to disappear."

Duncan straightened beside her. "Can we swing by Jackson, then hit the highway toward one of those larger cities?"

She tightened her grasp on his arm. "Duncan, both Laramie and Cheyenne are on the opposite side of the state without a lot of ways to get there. Wyoming is all about wide-open spaces."

He grimaced. "Okay, so what is the alternative? Fly out of Jackson?"

The two US marshals exchanged a look. "We might be able to make that an option," Slade said slowly. "The airport is tiny, but we can hire a private prop plane to get us out of there before anyone is the wiser."

"Could work," Colt agreed. "I'll make those arrangements."

The tension eased out of Duncan. "Good. I like that plan."

Chelsey frowned. "We're all going to fly out together?"

Duncan looked at her in surprise. "Why wouldn't we?"

"I just meant, you're free to go home anytime, Duncan." She had to force herself to stay the words. "I know you asked your boss for extra time off work, but you have a life back in Milwaukee. A job, your family."

Duncan turned so that they were facing each other. "I'm not leaving you until I know you're safe, Chelsey."

Beyond Duncan's shoulder she could see the US marshals had moved off to the side to talk in private. No doubt, making plans about when to cut Duncan loose.

She'd always known it would happen sooner or later. Her desire to have him stay was her problem, not his. The only good thing about entering witness protection was that she wasn't leaving her parents behind. She didn't have siblings, and no extended family, either.

"I don't want to leave you," Duncan said in a low voice.

The urge to throw herself into his arms was strong. It took every ounce of willpower she possessed to take one step back, then another.

"Excuse me, I need to find the bathroom." A lame excuse, maybe, but one that ensured Duncan wouldn't try to follow her.

She ducked into the bathroom, closing the door firmly behind her. Now that the point of losing Duncan forever was near, she could hardly bear it.

Tears threatened. She swiped at her eyes and took several deep breaths in an attempt to ward them off.

She splashed cold water on her face to hide the evidence of her distress, burying her face in a towel that smelled of laundry soap.

Enough. She'd be fine. She'd do this. God would show her the way.

Bolstered by the thought, she straightened her shoulders and opened the door. A dark shape caught the corner of her eye. Someone was in the bedroom!

"Duncan!" As his name left her lips, a man lunged at her, his strong hands digging into her flesh. She clawed at him, hoping and praying he didn't have a gun.

Duncan rushed forward first, followed by the two marshals. They quickly wrestled the guy off her, pinning him to the floor.

She eased backward, her heart hammering in her chest, her breathing uneven. Being grabbed like that had been more frightening than being shot at from a distance. She lifted a trembling hand to finger the fresh scratches on her face and neck.

If she hadn't caught a glimpse of him, he would have gotten to her before she could react. If he'd gotten her out of the cabin, where would they have gone?

She didn't want to imagine how that scenario might have played out.

"Who are you? Who sent you?" Duncan peppered the guy with questions as Slade tossed the guy's weapon aside and yanked his arms behind him to handcuff his wrists. Colt went into the bedroom where they guy had gotten in through a window, and quickly locked the door to prevent anyone else from getting inside.

The man sneered but didn't say a word.

"You'll want to cooperate with us," Slade said in a low voice. "Think about it for a moment. I'm sure that gun of yours will match ballistics of at least one unsolved crime, maybe more, which means you're going to be in federal prison for a long, long time."

The guy muttered something harsh and nasty under his breath.

"See, that's not going to help you," Slade drawled. "Let's try again. Who are you and who hired you to come after Chelsey?"

The captured guy didn't speak for a long moment. Finally he said, "I'm just a low man on the totem pole."

"Yeah, we already figured that out," Duncan said in a harsh tone. "After all, you failed to get Chelsey, didn't you? Once we put your mug shot out there for everyone to see, your boss will know you've failed him."

The guy's face turned beet red. "Fine,

it was Wesley Strand who hired me to get the girl."

"To get the girl? Or to kill her?" Duncan asked.

The guy turned and looked directly at Chelsey. A ripple of fear skittered down her spine at the sheer hatred in his eyes.

Never in her life had she been targeted by men who didn't hesitate to kill to get what they wanted.

But looking at this man, she knew he'd intended to kill her. And that he was only sorry about getting caught.

TWELVE

"To get her, or kill her?" Duncan repeated. It wasn't easy to control his anger when he saw the marks this jerk had left on Chelsey's face and neck.

The assailant shrugged. "Doesn't matter."

It did matter to Duncan, very much. He stared at the guy, trying to mesh his face with that of the man who'd assaulted him on the side of the mountain. But he was certain they weren't the same.

"Your team failed several times now," Duncan said. "And we've always gotten the upper hand, right? I'm pretty sure Wesley Strand isn't going to be impressed at how your cohort failed to kill us."

Their perp looked away, and Duncan

knew the guy didn't like being reminded of his shortcomings.

"You don't want to talk? That's fine," Slade drawled. "We can book you for one count of assault and battery against Chelsey. When we find the others, we'll add conspiracy to commit murder."

A flicker of concern shadowed the guy's gaze but then vanished. "Whatever."

"You're going to jail," Slade said. "You can either choose to cooperate or do the time, makes no difference to me." He jerked the guy to his feet. "Let's put him in the spare bedroom, the one he didn't breach, until we can hand him over to the authorities."

Duncan stepped back to give Slade room. Colt was still standing guard in the hallway between the two bedrooms, just in case someone else tried the same trick.

Duncan stood for a moment, willing his heart rate to return to normal. Then he approached Chelsey, lifting his palm to cup her cheek. "I'm sorry he hurt you."

"I'm fine." Chelsey's stricken expression contradicted her claim, so he gently pulled her into his arms. She melted against him, burying her face against his chest. He lightly stroked her soft curls. "This will never stop, will it?"

"It will stop if we find and arrest the people involved." Starting, he thought, with Wesley Strand and ultimately nailing Anthony Nettles.

Not to mention whatever role millionaire Travis Wolfe played in this. Too many suspects and not enough evidence.

Chelsey clung to him for a long time, then pulled herself together. She tipped her head back to gaze up at him. "Thanks, Duncan. For being my rock through this."

"I'm glad to be here for you." His voice was low and gravelly, and he cleared his throat to cover the emotional roller coaster he was experiencing. He cared about Chelsey, far more than he should.

Knowing they had so little time together didn't help.

She stepped back and drew a hand through her hair. "Before you ask, I've never heard Brett talk about anyone by the name of Wesley Strand."

He drew her into the kitchen, nudging her into a chair. "Let's see if we can find him online."

Slade and Colt returned to the kitchen wearing grim expressions. "We've secured the two bedrooms as best we can for now. We need to turn this guy over to the authorities, but we're not exactly sure who to trust," Slade said. "If there's a leak in the Jackson Police Department, I'm afraid this guy will slip away."

Duncan glanced up. "What about the park rangers? The attack on me was in the Grand Teton National Park, doesn't that give them some jurisdiction? We know this guy is working with the guy who attacked me."

"We can't prove he's part of the attack on the mountain, but the park rangers have a jail." Slade shrugged. "But they mostly hold criminals until the local law enforcement agency can take custody."

"Maybe we can convince Ranger Eric Connolly to hang on to him for a few days," Duncan suggested.

"It would be great if they'd hold him long enough to run his fingerprints through the database to get an ID," Slade said.

"He refuses to say anything else without his lawyer," Colt added. "I'm surprised he gave us Wesley Strand's name."

"Yeah, except he could very well be lying," Duncan said. "I'm trying to pull up information on Wesley Strand now."

The marshals crowded around him to see the screen, the only sound from the tapping of computer keys. Images bloomed on the screen, and he quickly narrowed his search to include Anthony Nettles and Travis Wolfe.

Bingo. A photo came up showing Anthony Nettles standing in front of a building with Travis Wolfe and Wolfe's chief of security, Wesley Strand.

"Got him." Duncan blew up the image on the screen and turned the computer toward Chelsey. "Does this guy look familiar?"

She wrinkled her forehead. "No."

"Head of security for Travis Wolfe?" Slade echoed. "That's interesting."

"If it's true he really set up the hit," Duncan cautioned. "We can only trust the guy so far."

Colt let out a heavy sigh. "Okay, let's just say our perp is telling the truth. How does that fit in with the idea of organized crime? If Wolfe is already a multimillionaire, why does he need to get involved with Coyote Creek Construction?"

"Maybe crime is how he got to be so rich," Slade said thoughtfully. "We know that organized crime rings often have legitimate businesses intermingled with their illegal activities. It's the best way to launder money."

"But they also typically stay off the

radar," Duncan pointed out. "Rather than flaunt their wealth."

The group fell silent, as they pondered the impact of what they'd learned.

Finally, Chelsey spoke up. "I still think we need to get to the Teton Valley Hotel to find Brett's folder."

Duncan glanced at her. "You have a point. The fact that this guy took a chance in slipping into the cabin in broad daylight reeks of desperation. The sooner we get out of Moose, Wyoming, the better."

Colt and Slade exchanged a glance. "It would be better to wait until dark," Colt pointed out. "But I agree, staying here doesn't seem to be a good plan."

"I'll call Ranger Connolly. Maybe he has an idea of where we can hide out for a while." Slade stepped away with his phone.

Duncan understood where the marshals were coming from. Obviously, getting out of town would be best after dark, at least as far as making it difficult for anyone to follow them. But two attempts here in the cabin over the past couple of hours wasn't good, either.

Resting his hands on Chelsey's shoulders, he tried not to count down the hours that he had left with her. Less than twenty-four hours for sure. From his army experience he knew flying in small planes close to the mountains at night was extremely dangerous. The earliest Chelsey would be able to be flown out of Jackson was early tomorrow morning.

Eighteen hours. A wave of helplessness washed over him.

After attempting to keep an emotional distance from her, he was forced to admit eighteen hours wasn't nearly enough.

Not when he longed for so much more.

Chelsey sat at the kitchen table, listening as they made their plans for the next few hours. Duncan was unusually silent, and she wondered what he was thinking.

"Connolly and Davidson will be here

shortly," Slade announced. "Davidson offered up his place for us to use."

"That's very nice of him," Chelsey said.

"I just hope his place is isolated from the others," Duncan said, breaking his silence. "I saw a long apartment building on our way in."

"I don't know where he lives," Slade said. "But at this point being surrounded by other rangers might not be so bad. At least they have law enforcement training and weapons."

She'd noticed Colt went back to keeping watch over their captured assailant. She shivered, remembering the feel of his hands grasping at her, his hot breath on her face.

Maybe getting out of here was the best option. Why wait until darkness when the threats had been nonstop?

The two park rangers arrived a few minutes later. Duncan carefully checked the door before letting them inside.

"The man who assaulted Chelsey is in

the spare bedroom. We have reason to believe he's part of the team who tried to shoot us in the mountains." He jerked a thumb over his shoulder. "US Marshal Colt Nelson is watching over him now."

"Okay," Eric said with a nod. "We'll lock your guy up first, then we'll relocate all of you to Davidson's place. He's the only one who has a home here. The rest of us use the apartment building on the other end of town."

"I want you both to know how much I appreciate what you're doing for me," Chelsey said. "This is above and beyond the call of duty."

Paul Davidson shrugged off her gratitude. "Not at all, it's our job. I don't like men shooting at civilians in my park."

The process took longer than Chelsey had imagined, but ninety minutes later, they were ready to leave. As before, Duncan and Slade shielded Chelsey with their bodies as they left the cabin, Slade disabling the alarm so they could tuck her safely in the back seat of the SUV. She was secretly glad when Duncan slid in beside her, leaving Slade and Colt up front.

Duncan took her hand, his fingers warmly curling around hers. She clung to him, hating knowing their time together would end soon.

"Hey, check out that van up ahead," Slade said from the front seat.

Chelsey craned her neck to see. Her jaw dropped when she realized the van was familiar, all white with tan lettering along the side, three capital letter *C*s, then in smaller lettering, the words *Coyote Creek Construction*.

"Let's follow it," Colt suggested.

"It might be better to grab the driver and question him," Duncan pointed out. "See how slow it's moving? He might be out here looking for the guy who we just hauled off to jail for attacking Chelsey."

"There's only one road, so it's not like I have any other option than to stay behind him," Slade pointed out.

"He's slowing down," Colt said, a hint of anticipation in his voice. "Maybe we should grab him."

"He could just be a construction worker for the company," Chelsey felt the need to point out.

"What's he doing in Moose?" Duncan asked. "I highly doubt there's any new construction going on here. This town is unincorporated, there isn't much to draw people to living here, unless they're working for the park service, the hotel or the restaurant."

She had to admit Duncan was right. But she also didn't like the idea of hassling an innocent man.

"He's turning into the gas station," Colt said. "Grabbing him while he's filling his tank is our best option."

"Let's do it," Slade agreed.

Chelsey tightened her grip on Duncan's hand, hoping he wouldn't volunteer. She could tell he wanted to but remained at her side.

Slade pulled in behind the van, then the two marshals waited until the driver was pumping gas before getting out of the SUV and surrounding him.

There were no raised voices, but from the body language, it was clear the van driver was protesting his innocence. Duncan slid his window down a bit so they could hear.

"I don't know anything about Wesley Strand," the driver said. "Or about any plan to kill anyone."

"That's not your buddy's story," Slade said. "He's singing like a bird."

The driver flinched and tried to jump into the van, but the marshals had him surrounded. This time it was Colt who used his handcuffs while Slade came back to the SUV.

"Colt is going to take this guy to the rangers' jail, too," he informed them.

"But—he hasn't committed a crime, has he?" Chelsey asked.

"He's armed and has no driver's license on him and is refusing to give us his name," Slade said. "They can hold him for driving without a license until we can identify him but may also charge him with conspiracy to commit murder. From there, local law enforcement can take over."

She let out a frustrated sigh. "You mean the ones we don't trust."

Slade shrugged. "It gets him off the streets for a while, maybe even long enough for us to get you transferred safely out of Wyoming."

Out of Wyoming. A hard lump formed in her throat. She forced a nod, then sat back to watch as Colt pushed the hand-cuffed man into the Coyote Creek Construction van and finish filling the tank. Colt took the van, while Slade climbed into the SUV. Ranger Davidson was waiting for them in front of his house.

"It's nothing fancy," Paul said, opening the front door. "But it should be safe enough until nightfall. Oh, and I have these for you." He gestured to several dark vests hanging over the backs of his kitchen chairs.

"Bullet-resistant vests?" Duncan moved over to lift one up. "Nice, but I'm surprised the park rangers have them."

"They're several years old. We got them for an incident a while back when a group of poachers began shooting at us." Paul scowled. "Shot a friend of mine. He survived but can't work as a ranger anymore."

"I'm sorry to hear that," Chelsey murmured. "I had no idea being a park ranger could be so dangerous."

"Normally it's not that bad, but there are always times like this when things heat up." Paul reached out to pick up a vest. "This is the smallest one we have, so I thought it would be good for you, Chelsey."

Duncan reached over to take the vest. "Let me help you get this on."

The vest was black and heavier than she imagined. It was difficult to comprehend how she'd gone from being a bride at her wedding to hiding out from bad guys wearing a bulletproof vest in the span of two days.

It felt like a lifetime.

Duncan pulled his vest on, then turned toward Paul. "US Marshal Colt Nelson is taking the driver of the Coyote Creek Construction van to sit in your jail. We believe he's the assailant's partner."

"Two men down, then," Slade mused. "And how many more out there?"

Chelsey shivered, not really wanting to know.

Duncan fingered his vest for a moment, then turned toward Slade. "I have an idea. Maybe I can pretend to be one of them enough to draw others out of hiding."

"No way." Chelsey couldn't help her instinctive response. "That's a dangerous idea. Besides, why would they mistake you for one of them?"

"Why wouldn't they?" Duncan asked. "I can dress in black from head to toe, like they did, and keep my head down, maybe wear a bandanna around my neck. They wouldn't know the difference until they got close enough."

"And then what?" Twines of panic reached up to circle her throat. "They kill you?"

"I can hold my own," Duncan said.

Slade cleared his throat. "I don't think that's a good idea, Duncan. Let's keep our heads down for now, and work on a plan to get inside the Teton Valley Hotel." He looked at her. "I've changed my mind about you coming along. I think we'll need your help with the hotel layout, Chelsey. We need to know the best way to sneak in and out of the place."

Duncan didn't give up his idea so easily. "Don't you think getting rid of anyone else out there watching for Chelsey is our best way of getting to the hotel without being followed?"

Slade narrowed his gaze in frustration. "No, I don't think you risking your life is our best chance. I'm sure whoever is behind this already has men lined up to replace the two we've taken out of commission."

"Okay, fine. Chelsey, have a seat." Duncan guided her to the closest chair. "We'll work on a plan for getting Brett's folder, if it's still there."

"It will be," Chelsey said, striving to remain positive.

"Paul, we need paper and pencil to draw a map of the hotel," Slade said.

The ranger brought over the supplies. Chelsey thought about the hotel and began to draw a basic outline of the building.

"The main entrances are here, here and here." She drew squares to indicate the areas. "But we bring our supplies in through the loading dock which is located here." She indicated a spot in the back of the building. "And the employee entrance is back there, too, next to the area where the trucks pull up to unload." She drew a smaller door a short distance from the loading dock.

"All the employees go in that way?" Duncan asked.

"Not all, but the kitchen crew and the cleaning staff do. The restaurant servers and front desk staff come in through the main entrance. But going in through the loading dock makes it easy to get to my office located down the hall to the right."

"There must be other ways inside that guests might use," Slade said, gesturing to her rudimentary drawing.

"Yes, accessed with their room key cards." She quickly marked them, then glanced up. "But I hardly think anyone from Coyote Creek Construction would have a guest key."

"They would if they booked a room for the wedding." Duncan's tone was grim.

She nodded slowly. "I guess you're right about that. But Trish, my assistant manager, would make sure to deactivate those keys once they've checked out."

"If they've checked out." Duncan sighed. "I'm getting the feeling that sneaking into the building will be more difficult than I anticipated. After all, hotels are open 24/7 to their guests. We can try to sneak in, but who's to say others won't be wandering around as well?"

Her heart squeezed in her chest. The plan that had sounded so simple now took on a whole new level of complexity.

But she wasn't about to let that deter her from going along. If Brett's honeymoon folder was there, she wanted to see for herself what he might have as evidence.

Before the marshals whisked her away to start a new life under a new name in a place where she'd be surrounded by strangers.

THIRTEEN

While waiting for darkness to fall, Duncan continued using Slade's computer in an attempt to investigate the murder that started all of this.

The killing of Roland Perry.

Duncan had tried to find something on Roland Perry before but had come up empty-handed. Now he tried again, using the Wyoming DMV access provided by Ranger Paul Davidson.

There. He finally got a match. Roland Perry had a Wyoming driver's license with an address listed in Cheyenne.

Excited to have a lead, he searched for the address. Then frowned at the screen when the building that popped up was an old abandoned store.

"What's wrong?" Chelsey asked.

"I found a guy named Roland Perry, but the address in Cheyenne is an old abandoned building." He turned the screen to show her the small and less than flattering DMV photo. According to the license, Roland Perry was five feet ten inches tall, weighed 175 pounds, had brown eyes and light brown hair. His date of birth was listed November 12 and he was thirty-six years old. "I don't suppose he looks familiar?"

Chelsey scooted her chair closer for a better look. She stared at the image for a long moment. "Maybe," she finally admitted. "I just can't remember where."

A spurt of adrenaline hit. "Was it possible he was in the hotel dining room with the rich guy, too?"

She grimaced. "No, I don't think so. I seem to remember him wearing dusty jeans, T-shirt and steel-toed boots, as if he was one of the construction workers."

"When would you have seen one of the construction workers?" Duncan asked.

Her expression cleared. "I remember now—he was one of the guys Brett brought over when we were discussing the plans for the hotel expansion." She pulled the drawing over. "See, we were thinking of adding a wing to the north, this way, with high-end suites. I don't remember this guy going by the name of Roland Perry, though. I think he was introduced to me as Ray."

Ray as a nickname to Roland? Maybe. "You think he actually worked boots on the ground for Coyote Creek Construction?"

She nodded. "Yes, but I have to say, he seemed to be more interested in the hotel itself, asking me about my parents and how long we owned it. He seemed interested in the fact that our hotel once belonged to my grandparents, and my great-grandparents before that. He also asked a lot of questions about Elroy Lansing's land." She frowned. "You really think this is the man who was murdered?"

Duncan didn't believe in coincidences, and this one was no exception. "According to his driver's license it appears that way. But I still don't exactly understand why he'd be viewed as a threat enough to murder him."

"Maybe Brett was wrong about who he saw that night," Chelsey said.

There was no denying Brett had lied to them more than once. But the local police had also claimed no one had seen the guy in a few days. And other than a fake address and a driver's license it seemed the guy didn't exist anywhere else online, certainly not on social media.

What did it all mean?

It still bothered him that the rich guy, Travis Wolfe, might be involved. He wished there was a way to bring Wesley Strand in for questioning. In his experience, loyalty to a boss went only so far when you were the one faced with doing jail time.

But he wasn't the cop in charge here. Just a concerned citizen trying to keep an innocent woman safe.

"Find something?" Slade asked, entering the kitchen.

Duncan quickly filled the marshal in on what he'd found about Roland or Ray Perry, including Chelsey's meeting with him and Brett at the hotel.

"You're right, it doesn't make any sense." Slade sighed. "Let me make more calls, going higher up the chain this time to find more about this guy's identity," Slade said. "The last time I checked, we were told the guy didn't exist, but that's clearly not the case if you found a driver's license for the guy. There's something fishy going on here, and I don't like it."

Duncan silently agreed. He thought for a moment about how he'd tried to go undercover, not taking a new identity, but pretending to be someone he wasn't in an effort to identify who had killed Max Callahan, the Milwaukee chief of police and patriarch of the Callahan family. It wasn't an easy task, that was for sure.

Could this Ray or Roland Perry have been doing something similar? There was no evidence that he was anything other than a construction worker, except for the fact that Brett claimed he was murdered.

And normal, average, everyday construction guys didn't get murdered for no good reason.

He really, really wanted to see what, if any, evidence Brett actually had in his honeymoon folder.

Slade was on the phone for a long time, listening without saying much. Duncan sensed that he was being sent higher up the chain and wondered what that meant.

"Duncan?" Chelsey's voice pulled him from his thoughts.

"What is it?" He leaned forward to take her hand in his. The ache in his chest intensified at the thought of not seeing her again after tomorrow. Even though they'd been reconnected for only a short time—days, really, since the moment Brett had been murdered—he felt as if he would be leaving a piece of his heart behind.

Not that Chelsey had asked for his heart. Or even indicated that she felt the same toward him. Despite having expressed her doubts about marrying Brett, he didn't think she was interested in jumping into another relationship, with anyone.

Including him.

And that had been okay, at first, but now? Despite his efforts he realized his feelings toward Chelsey had become... complicated.

"When we go to the hotel, we should look through Brett's room, in case I'm wrong about the honeymoon folder."

"I agree, although it seems to me that hiding the photos in plain sight, so to speak, would be a smart thing to do. How many bad guys would look there for evidence?"

"Do you think they killed Brett because of the evidence?" Her expression was grave. "I'm worried Trish is in danger just by being my assistant hotel manager."

"I don't know, Chelsey. At this point, we have to expect the worst, while hoping for the best."

"While praying for God to watch over us," she added.

He drew in a deep breath. "My sister, Shayla, and her husband, Mike Callahan, are believers." He offered a wry smile. "I've attended some church services with them, but I wish I had made more of an effort to understand their faith."

"Many people keep their faith private, but you need to know that leaning on God is the only thing keeping me going." She tightened her grip on his hand. "Maybe, once you go back home, you'll attend services, as a way to remember me."

"Chels," he whispered her name through a throat thick with emotion. "Of course

I'll do that, but I won't ever forget you. That's a promise."

Her blue eyes glittered with tears, but then she swiped at her face and looked away. "It would be better for you to forget me, Duncan. We'll both have to find a way to move on when this is over."

No way. He'd never forget her, ever. For a moment he thought about joining her in WITSEC. Then he thought about his dad, and his sister, Shayla, and her two kids, Brodie and Breena. His heart squeezed painfully.

Give them up? His entire family? Never to see them again?

Yet leaving Chelsey was beginning to ache the same way as when he'd lost Amanda.

"I don't believe it," Slade said with frustration.

He pulled himself from his troublesome thoughts. Slade looked mad, which was unusual at least in the short time he'd come to know the guy. "What?"

"Roland Perry was an undercover cop." Slade shook his head with disgust. "He was assigned to infiltrate the construction company in an attempt to find evidence of criminal activity."

A cop? A chill snaked down his spine and suddenly it all made sense. "Okay, but why in the world didn't they tell you that when you learned Brett witnessed his murder?"

"Apparently Roland Perry's status was on a *need to know basis*, and my job as Brett's handler wasn't enough to put me in that group." There was no mistaking the bitterness in Slade's tone.

"Nettles killed an undercover cop." Duncan sighed. "We better hope Brett wasn't lying about that, and that he really did have evidence." He met Slade's gaze. "We can't let a cop killer walk."

"I know." Slade's voice held a note of resignation. "And I'd love nothing more than to prevent that from happening, but you have to understand my main job for the foreseeable future is to protect Chelsey."

Duncan knew that all too well. He wanted to be the one to protect her, but soon he'd be forced to hand her over to Slade Brooks permanently.

If Chelsey was right about God's plan, then maybe his role was to help solve the crime. After all, that was what cops like him did. Arrest the bad guys and toss them in jail.

If that was all he could do for Chelsey, then he wouldn't rest until he'd accomplished that task.

Chelsey forced herself to put some distance between her and Duncan. She had to stop leaning on him like this. The sooner she figured out how to manage on her own, the better.

Duncan couldn't assist with her transition into her new life. Apparently, that was Slade's job.

She tried to take solace that she wouldn't

be alone, but knew it wouldn't be the same. Slade was a nice guy, handsome and dedicated, but he wasn't Duncan.

Her feelings toward Duncan were spiraling out of control. Worse than the way she'd fallen so quickly for Brett after her mother's death. She knew that these tender feelings she had for Duncan might not be real, but over the past two days, she'd learned he was far more honorable than Brett.

Which still didn't mean she was falling in love with him. Not like the tepid feelings she'd had for Brett, but for real.

The way her parents had loved each other for over thirty years.

"Colt is bringing pizza for dinner," Slade said. "With daylight savings time, I'd like to wait until ten o'clock before heading over to Jackson."

"At least we have a few clouds rolling in," Duncan pointed out. "The quarter moon shouldn't be too much of a problem."

"We'll drive without lights until we're

out on the highway," Slade agreed. "From there we should be okay."

Chelsey tried not to worry too much about getting out of Moose and to the Teton Valley Hotel. Of more concern was what they would, or wouldn't, find there.

Hearing that Nettles had killed an undercover cop was sobering. Had the murder been done because they'd uncovered his real identity? Or because they'd simply found him snooping around? Murder seemed a drastic punishment for snooping, but if organized crime was involved, she doubted they let little things like morals get in the way.

The evening hours went by slowly. The pizza was good, and the guys seemed relaxed as they sat around her at the table. It was almost as if they were just hanging out, rather than getting prepared for a dangerous expedition.

Exhaustion began to weigh her down at about nine o'clock. Duncan urged her to stretch out on the sofa for a while. She didn't argue. Better to get a little nap in now, in preparation for what could be a long night.

She didn't think she'd really get any rest, but she must have dozed because Duncan's hand on her shoulder gently shook her awake. "Chels? It's time."

Blinking away the remnants of sleep, she sat up, adjusted the bulky bullet-resistant vest and nodded. "Okay."

Slade, Colt and Duncan escorted her outside. There weren't streetlights in Moose, but lights were visible from various apartment windows. The mountains behind them were nothing but dark shadows, and she hoped that meant that anyone lurking there wouldn't be able to see them clearly, either.

"What if they have night vision goggles?" she whispered as they headed outside.

"We've got you covered, Chelsey," Duncan assured her. "Besides, the assailant on the mountain didn't have them and neither did the guy who broke into the cabin. As much as they think they're professionals, they wouldn't have lasted long in Afghanistan."

Slade eyed him thoughtfully. "You served over there?"

Duncan nodded, but didn't elaborate.

She slid into the back seat of the SUV, followed by Duncan. The two marshals sat in front, and as planned, Slade drove out of the driveway without using his lights.

A tense silence reigned inside the vehicle, but after ten minutes and reaching the highway without a problem, the guys relaxed a bit.

Chelsey rested against Duncan. He kissed the top of her head, and she tried not to remember the heat of his kiss. Slade made exceptionally good time getting to Jackson. As they headed toward Teton Valley Hotel, Chelsey straightened and looked around.

She wasn't sure what she'd expected, maybe dozens of police vehicles still surrounding the place, but everything looked normal.

As if a groom being shot just before his wedding had never happened.

Slade hit the lights as they approached the hotel. Her map must have been pretty good, because Slade found the service drive leading to the loading dock without difficulty.

Tension returned as Slade, Duncan and Chelsey eased out of the SUV. Colt was designated to stay with the SUV and to watch the back door and the road. Large garbage dumpsters were located back there, too, and Chelsey wrinkled her nose at the ripe scent.

The guys didn't seem to notice. With Duncan in the front, and Slade behind her, they made their way up toward the employee-only entrance. Chelsey punched in the key code and the door opened with a click.

No one spoke as they went inside. Duncan walked in front of her, so she gently pushed him in the direction of her office. The hour wasn't that late, going on eleven thirty at night, but there was no sound of activity coming from the area of the lobby.

Chelsey fought her instinct to go find out what was going on. Had the hotel lost business after the wedding fiasco? Had people cancelled their reservations because of the violence?

She reminded herself it didn't matter, because she wasn't going to be managing the hotel anymore. Upon reaching her office door, she tried the knob, belatedly realizing she didn't have a key.

What bride carried her keys down the aisle?

The door was locked. She looked up at Duncan in horror. He glanced at Slade and nodded. The US marshal nudged her aside then pulled some tools out of his pocket and went to work.

She'd never watched anyone pick a lock before and was impressed at how easy Slade made it look. A minute later, he pushed the office door open. Duncan went in first, with Chelsey directly behind him.

Not until Slade closed the door behind him did Duncan use the penlight Ranger Paul Davidson had given him. He made a wide arc with the light, verifying there was no one else in the office.

Eerily, the place looked as if she'd just left it. Maybe Trish was waiting for her to return. Chelsey instinctively moved to her desk and the stack of folders sitting off to the right. She lifted them, searching for the yellow honeymoon folder that she remembered Brett tucking under the pile.

It was gone.

"What's wrong?" Duncan whispered.

"The folder isn't where I expected it to be." Her stomach knotted painfully, and she quickly began to search the entire desktop.

The folder had to be here, it just had to be!

"Which room was Brett using?" Duncan

asked. "I can check the place out while you keep searching here."

"Room 112, but I don't have a key and I don't think your lock picks will work on the room doors." She shifted another stack of papers aside. "I know the folder is here somewhere."

"Should I check the file drawers?" Slade offered.

She shook her head, trying to ignore the pounding of her heart. "Duncan? Shine your light here, please."

Duncan came up to stand behind her, so that she could see her desk. A glint of yellow caught her eye and she shoved the pad of paper aside and uncovered the folder. "Got it."

"Let's see what's inside." Slade came up to stand beside her. Duncan kept the narrow beam of the flashlight centered on the folder as she opened it up.

The photograph on top was an ad for an exclusive honeymoon resort. She shoved it aside without a second glance, riffling through the rest of the contents. It wasn't until the back of the folder that she found two photographs.

The picture was a little grainy, but not enough that she couldn't make out two men standing in a large building filled with boxes that appeared to be labeled with the Coyote Creek Construction logo. One man, a guy who looked vaguely like the picture of Anthony Nettles, held a gun and was clearly threatening the other man who she now recognized as Roland Perry. The second picture showed the man with the gun, and Perry lying on the ground in a dark pool of blood.

"That's it," Duncan said in a low, hoarse voice.

"I can't believe he kept this from us," Slade whispered harshly. "If he'd have turned this over to me right away, he'd still be alive."

"Take them." She stepped away from the desk. "I'm just glad we found them."

Slade picked up the folder when his cell

phone buzzed. He glanced at the screen and quickly answered. "Colt? What's wrong?"

It was so quiet in the office it was easy to hear Colt's response. "We have company. Black truck just pulled in."

Chelsey froze and glanced at Duncan. "I know this hotel like the back of my hand. We'll find a way out."

"Colt? Stay out of sight. We'll be in touch." Slade disconnected from the call. "All right, Chelsey. Let's go."

Swallowing her fear, she gently turned the knob of her office door and cracked it open. For the first time since Brett's murder, she was responsible for the lives of these two men.

A heavy burden. *Please, Lord, show me the way!*

FOURTEEN

Duncan put a hand on Chelsey's shoulder, preventing her from going out of the office. He lowered his mouth to her ear. "Me first. Tell me which way to go."

She shook her head. "Too difficult to navigate. Follow me."

He didn't like it, but arguing was a waste of time they didn't have. It seemed as if their planned late-night escape from Moose had only postponed being found by the bad guys, not circumvented it.

They should have gotten in and out of Chelsey's office as quickly as possible.

Over Chelsey's shoulder he could see the hallway was deserted and quiet. She moved out and headed in the opposite direction from which they'd come in. He tensed, hoping she wasn't planning to take them to the front door.

She didn't. Instead, she turned down another hallway, going past a couple of conference rooms that were thankfully empty. She turned right and led them down a narrow hallway with hotel room doors located on either side.

It was pretty quiet for a hotel, although thinking back, he realized the wedding was on Saturday so that meant today was Monday. Not as much going on, apparently even in June.

"Colt? What's happening?" Slade asked softly. "We're heading toward the north end of the building."

"See you soon." In the quiet hallway Duncan could hear Colt's muffled response without the phone being on speaker.

Duncan glanced over his shoulder at Slade. "He didn't answer your question."

Slade gave a curt nod. "I know."

At the end of the hallway, there was a door leading outside to a flat parking lot.

Once again, he rested his hand on her shoulder to prevent her from going outside. "Wait for Colt."

She nodded and peered through the glass door. From what he could see of the parking lot, there was a scattering of cars on the left, all of them close to the door. For whatever reason, there weren't many cars parked on the right. Maybe they were parked closer to their rooms, overlooking the mountains.

The hotel was located in a valley— the mountains circled the property on all sides—which is why the loading dock was tucked away in the back of the building.

There was a niggling itch along the back of his neck, a sixth sense telling him something wasn't right. They'd gotten the evidence against Anthony Nettles but needed to stay alive long enough to use it.

A dark shape came around the corner from the right side of the building.

Chelsey pushed against the door, but he held her back, waiting. Slade's phone vibrated.

"That you, Colt? Okay, we're coming," Slade said.

The SUV rolled to a stop right across from the door. Duncan nudged Chelsey aside so he could go first. Less than a minute later, they were in the back seat of the SUV.

Colt drove slowly, going around the corner, then pulling up into a parking spot between two other cars. He shut down the engine, then turned to look at them. "I think we need to stay down for a while, long enough for the black truck to leave."

"Good idea," Slade said. "We'll stay low."

Duncan made sure Chelsey was crouched behind the passenger seat before doing the same.

They'd been settled in their hiding spots for only five minutes when bright headlights slowly swept past them. No one moved or spoke. Duncan had no doubt the vehicle would take a second pass, maybe even a third before leaving.

Unless…he swallowed hard. What if they decided to go from car to car searching for them? It wouldn't take long to uncover their hiding spot. He found himself praying they wouldn't. Praying didn't come naturally to him, but he bowed his head so his chin was resting on his chest.

Please, Lord, guide us through this danger.

Chelsey shifted, ever so slightly. He glanced over and whispered, "You okay?"

"Yes." A second later, the headlights washed over them again.

He didn't like it. "Colt? We may have to make a run for it. I'm worried they'll send someone to search each vehicle on foot. The alarm won't help if they have a gun."

"Already on it," Colt answered. "I timed their sweep. In two minutes, I'm going to get us out of here. You and Chelsey need to stay down."

"Okay." Duncan flashed an encouraging look at Chelsey. "We can do this."

She nodded. "With God's help."

"Yes." There wasn't time to say anything more as Colt fired up the engine and backed out of the parking spot. From Duncan's position behind the driver's seat, he couldn't tell if Colt was using his headlights or not.

Colt didn't waste any time but headed straight out of the parking lot back out onto the highway. "Slade? Ideas on where to go from here? Take interstate 191 southeast or go off on the less traveled highway 20?"

"Stay on the main highway, more traffic that way."

Traffic? Duncan swallowed a protest. Wyoming didn't have traffic. Not like Chicago and other big cities did. "Don't forget you're flying Chelsey out of Jackson Hole Airport in the morning." He peered at his watch, his stomach clenching at the time. Midnight. "Which is only eight hours from now."

"Turn here," Slade said with urgency.

Colt cranked the wheel, taking a hard right. "Why?"

"Duncan's right, we need to stay in Jackson. I know there are a couple of hotels roughly seven to eight miles from the airport."

"Okay, but we'll need to find a place to hide the vehicle," Colt said. "If they start searching parking lots, they may recognize this one."

"Understood," Slade agreed.

Duncan's back and knees were starting to protest the uncomfortable position, but he ignored the aches and pains, more concerned with how Chelsey was doing. "How much longer, Colt?"

"Ten minutes," the marshal responded.

"Thanks." He stared at Chelsey. Eight hours to go before she'd be flown out of Wyoming, for good. The SUV slowed, then made a couple of turns before coming to a stop within the designated timeline.

"Stay down until I can get a couple of rooms," Slade instructed before easing out of the passenger seat.

It didn't take long for Slade to obtain two connecting rooms. Duncan stayed behind Chelsey as they headed inside, glad that their ground-floor rooms had easy access in and out.

"I'll park the SUV somewhere safe," Colt said. "Don't worry about how long I'm gone. It'll take me a while to hike back from the resort."

Duncan walked Chelsey through the connecting door to her room. For a long moment, neither of them said anything, even though there was so much he wanted to tell her.

"I'm tired but not sure I'll be able to sleep," Chelsey confided, dropping onto the edge of the bed. "It's all been so surreal. I don't know anything about where I'll be at this time tomorrow."

He sat in the only chair in the room, across from her. "I wish there was a way you could stay."

She let out a heavy sigh. "I think we both know that's impossible. The fact that they followed us to the hotel proves they won't stop until they get what they want."

He was very much afraid she was right. "I don't think they know about the evidence—maybe they believe we were there to get your personal things."

"Maybe." Chelsey looked down at the floor. "It's hard to accept the inability to take personal photographs with me."

"I can grab them for you," he offered. "That way if things change down the road you'll know that you'll be able to have them back some day."

"Really?" The offer caused her face to light up. "I'd love that, thanks."

"No problem." He hesitated, thinking back once again to his family back in Milwaukee. His dad, who might be marrying

Maggie Callahan; his sister, Shayla, and her two kids. "I'll go with you, Chelsey."

"What?" She looked confused. "You mean to get me settled? That won't work, the location has to be secret to the point where Slade is the only one who will know where I am."

"No, I mean, we can go into WITSEC together. I care about you, Chelsey. You need a friend, and I don't want to lose you."

Her mouth dropped open, and hope flashed briefly in her eyes, before she shook her head. "No, Duncan, I can't ask that of you."

"You never asked, Chels. I'm offering." He knew doing this would bring his family pain, but his dad had Maggie, and Shayla had Mike and their kids. They would all go on with their lives.

"Oh, Duncan." Her eyes filled with tears. "That's the sweetest offer in the entire world, but I can't let you do this. I can't let you give up your family. Mine is gone, so the sacrifice isn't nearly as great. But your dad and your sister both need you."

"They'll be okay without me," he began, but she abruptly cut him off.

"No, Duncan. I'm not going to let you do this." She jumped up from her perch on the bed and moved away. "I need to get cleaned up. I'll see you in the morning, okay?"

He stared at her for a long moment, trying to read between the lines. Was she refusing because she didn't care for him? Or because she didn't want him in her life?

Before he could try to clarify, she went into the tiny bathroom and closed the door behind her.

Leaving him little choice but to return to the room he was sharing with the guys, his gut filled with dread, his heart heavy.

All too soon, Chelsey would be leaving him forever. The same way Amanda had. Only Amanda had died, while Chelsey was making a conscious decision to go.

And there wasn't anything he could do to change that.

* * *

Chelsey collapsed on the edge of the closed lid of the toilet, her hands shaking as she hung her head.

That Duncan would make such a selfless offer was mind-boggling. And worse? She'd wanted nothing more than to throw herself into his arms and accept his sacrifice.

Refusing him had been one of the most difficult things she'd ever done. But she also knew it was the right thing to do.

Her feelings for Duncan were difficult to decipher. She might be falling in love with him but didn't trust her feelings. She'd made a hasty decision with Brett and look where that had landed her.

Right in the middle of this mess.

Yet spending time with Duncan prior to the wedding had shown her the truth about her feelings toward Brett. She'd been very attracted to Duncan. So much so, she'd realized how much she cared about Brett as a friend, not as a husband.

But Duncan had served in the army, and it was his nature to be a protector. And he'd done an admirable job guarding her.

She wouldn't be here if not for his expertise.

There was also the fact that if she hadn't agreed to marry Brett, she wouldn't have met Duncan again. He'd come to stand up as Brett's best man. Duncan hadn't come to Wyoming specifically to see her.

Foolish to think Duncan had fallen in love with his best man's bride. Duncan was too honorable for that.

No, the best thing she could do for Duncan was to let him go. Allow him to return home to his family, friends and career.

She loved him enough to give him the life he deserved.

What was left of the night dragged on forever. Chelsey woke up almost every hour and finally gave up trying to sleep at about six in the morning. The sky was beginning to lighten, several puffy white clouds floating across the sky, although a darker rain cloud hovered over the Grand Tetons.

She'd taken the bullet-resistant vest off last night and was doing her best to re-place it over her dark blue cotton shirt when she heard a light rap on the con-necting door.

"Come in." She turned in time to see Duncan step over the threshold. "Hey. I could use some help here."

He set a bag of food on the table, then came over to adjust the vest. "I brought breakfast from the fast food place across the street."

"How did you know I was awake?"

He shrugged, avoiding her gaze. "Heard you moving around, the walls are pretty thin."

She nodded and tugged on the edge of the vest to shift it into a more comfortable position. "What's the plan? What time are we heading to the airport?"

"Slade wants you to get there early, but it won't take long. They're hoping to leave here about seven thirty." Duncan finished securing the vest and stepped back, tucking his hands into his front pockets. "They want me to take the first flight back to Milwaukee."

"You should," she agreed. "Nothing more you can do here."

He scowled. "Other than help bring Anthony Nettles to justice for murdering an undercover cop and figure out what role Wesley Strand and Travis Wolfe play in all of this, if any."

"Surprised you haven't become a detective for the MPD," she said keeping her tone light and teasing.

"I'm scheduled to take the detective exam next month," he admitted. "But I'd give that up if it meant I could stay here to bring these guys to justice."

She wondered if he really understood how he'd be forced into giving up his career if she'd accepted his offer to come with her. Another reason for her to remain strong. "Well, you'll bring other bad guys to justice in Milwaukee, which will be good, too."

He glanced away. "Please come eat your breakfast before it gets cold."

"Is there coffee?" She moved past him to pick up the bag of food.

"I'll make some." Duncan busied himself with the small coffee maker available in their rooms.

She sensed he was upset with her but didn't want to rehash the subject of his coming with her all over again. They had just over an hour together, and for the first time, she wasn't sure what to say.

Some things were better left unsaid.

"Were you serious about getting some of my personal items at the hotel?" she asked.

He brought over a cup of coffee, doctored with cream and sugar the way she liked it. "Yes. Tell me what you'd like me to have and I'll find a way."

"Not now, though, right? I mean, it's not safe to go back there yet."

He shrugged. "You're the one in danger, Chelsey, not me."

She took a bite of her breakfast sandwich, thinking back to the wedding. "Are you sure? I mean, it wouldn't be difficult for anyone to figure out you were the one helping me."

"So far the attempts have been specifically targeted at you," he pointed out. "And they can't kill all of us."

"Why not? From what I can tell, they haven't balked at killing anyone, not even an undercover cop."

He seemed to consider her point. "You may be right, and if that is the case, maybe I should be relocated with you."

She wanted very badly to agree, but forced herself to look him directly in the eye. "Is that what Slade and Colt say?"

"Not yet, but it may be the right thing to do, regardless."

There was no good response to that, so she remained silent. Slade poked his head into the room. "Chelsey? We'd like to be ready to go by seven thirty."

"I know. I'll be ready." She finished her breakfast and coffee, then stood. "Give me a few minutes and I'll be set."

Duncan nodded. She took her time washing her face and brushing her teeth. She tucked two bobby pins in place to keep her hair out of her eyes. Looking at her reflection in the mirror, she found herself wondering what name she'd be given. Did she have a choice about that or had Slade already created new identification documents for her?

Did it really matter? Chelsey Robards would cease to exist and some new woman would be born in her place.

When she emerged from the bathroom, she heard voices from next door. Crossing over to the adjoining room, she could tell Duncan was pressing his case to be relocated with her.

They stopped arguing when she came in. "Ready to go?" Slade asked.

"Yes." She glanced around. "Where's Colt?"

"He left a while ago to retrieve the SUV." Slade pulled out his phone. "He'll text when he's here."

As if on cue the phone in Slade's hand chirped.

"Sounds like our ride is here," Duncan said. "Let's go."

They left the motel room, once again Duncan leading the way, Slade walking behind her. The SUV was parked a couple of spots down from where their rooms were located. As they approached the vehicle, they heard a high-pitched scream.

"What in the world?" Duncan spun toward the sound. Chelsey stopped in her tracks, trying to understand what was happening.

Then something hit her square in the chest, with enough force to send her reeling backward. She hit the ground, pain reverberating across her chest and along the back of her head.

She didn't move, couldn't breathe. For an instant she wondered if she was dead, but the overwhelming pain seemed to indicate she was alive.

"She's hit! She's hit!" The panic in Duncan's voice was the last thing she remembered before darkness claimed her.

FIFTEEN

Duncan fell to his knees, throwing himself over Chelsey to protect her from the shooter even though he wasn't sure where the guy was hiding. He tensed, bracing for a second shot, even as he called, "Help me, she's been hit!"

Colt ran over from the SUV. "Check her pulse. Is she still with us?"

Duncan felt for a pulse, but his own heart was hammering so hard he couldn't be sure. "I don't know," he whispered hoarsely. "She's not moving."

"We need to get her back inside," Slade said in a low, urgent tone. "Colt, call an ambulance and then see if you can find the shooter."

Duncan barely heard what they were

saying, his gaze focused on Chelsey. He was afraid to move her, but more terrified not to. He gathered her limp body into his arms, and rose to his feet, mentally kicking himself for falling for the oldest trick in the book.

The scream had been a diversion intended to separate him from Chelsey. And it had worked.

He set her down on the bed, gently placing a pillow beneath her head. The back of her hair was damp with blood and the room spun crazily for a moment before righting itself.

Please, God, don't let Chelsey die!

The wail of sirens could be heard in the distance, but he kept his gaze on Chelsey's still form. He felt again for a pulse, and this time was reassured when he identified the faint beat of her heart.

He bowed his head and silently thanked God for sparing her.

"Check her vest—see if the bullet is still

imbedded there, or if it went through," Slade said.

He fingered the vest, easily finding the spot in the center of her chest where the bullet had penetrated the vest. Quickly removing the vest, he was doubly thankful to realize the bullet hadn't gone into her skin.

Although he knew the impact would leave a massive bruise, regardless. That she wasn't moving concerned him. "Chelsey? Can you hear me?"

Her eyelids fluttered open and she looked confused for a moment before her expression cleared. "Duncan? Wh-what happened?"

"You were shot." He held up the vest. "I'm sure your chest hurts, you may even have a few cracked ribs, but the vest saved your life."

"Yeah, hurts." Her eyelids drooped. "Head and chest…"

He glanced at Slade. "We'll need to get her to the local hospital."

"There's one not too far, but we might not want to go there," Slade said.

"Why? Just because you think the shooter will try to find her at the only hospital in this town?" Duncan felt his anger simmering to a boil. "I don't care. It's your job to get her the medical treatment she needs."

"Hear me out, Duncan," Slade said, holding up a hand. "What if we pretend she's dead?"

His anger quickly faded as he recognized the wisdom of that plan. "You mean, treat her as if she's dead, so that the shooter thinks he's finished the job?"

"Why not?" Slade shrugged. "Seems to me he must not have noticed the vest. Maybe because you were standing in front of her until the scream drew you out of the way. He only had a second to take the shot and she went down like a rock. He has no reason to believe he missed."

The reminder of how badly he'd failed to keep Chelsey safe burned, but he couldn't deny Slade's plan had merit. "I like it. But she still needs care."

"I'm okay." Chelsey's whisper had him turning toward her. "I'm okay with pretending to be dead if it helps keep the rest of you safe."

"Yeah, she has a point about that. The situation in general has been bothering me," Slade said. "I'm not sure why they haven't taken a shot at you, Colt and me. The shooter had plenty of time. He could have picked us off one by one without much effort."

"I had the same thought last night," Duncan admitted. "It didn't make sense that they kept going after Chelsey. If they thought Brett told her something in confidence, then they should assume she'd have shared that same information with the rest of us, right? So why keep going after her?"

Slade shook his head. "I'm not sure. But faking her death may help solve that problem." Slade turned toward Chelsey. "Who gets the Teton Valley Hotel after you're gone?"

Her brow furrowed. "It's a good question. The hotel has been in our family for generations, but I don't have any heirs or family left. If Brett was alive and we actually got married, there may have been a way for him to pass it along to his family, but I'm sure now it will simply go up for auction to the highest bidder."

"Travis Wolfe is a millionaire who has already bought up the adjoining ranch," Duncan said as the last piece of the puzzle fell into place. "The assailant at the cabin said that he was sent by Wesley Strand. Could it be because Wolfe wants the hotel, too?"

Slade nodded slowly. "Seems drastic, but maybe killing Brett first, followed by Chelsey, was a way for them to get rid of two problems at one time. Get rid of the witness and the hotel owner."

Duncan felt certain they were onto something. The photograph of Nettles killing the undercover cop was enough to open an investigation but having Brett's eyewitness testimony would have been necessary to prove Nettles took the shot. That only took care of Anthony Nettles, owner of Coyote Creek Construction. Yet there was nothing more than a business relationship between Nettles and Wolfe. There was no way to implicate the millionaire in the crime.

Was that how Wolfe had planned it all along? Was it possible Wolfe had paid someone off in the local police department and had learned about Brett's report of what he'd witnessed?

It was all starting to make sense, at least in theory. Proving any of it was another story.

The sirens were louder now, red lights flashing outside the hotel window. They were running out of time if they were going to pull off faking Chelsey's death.

He grabbed the blanket and pulled it up over Chelsey's head. Slade nodded and went to the door. He held up his credentials for the two EMTs.

"I'm sorry, but she's gone. We won't need your services," Slade told them.

The two EMTs glanced at each other and frowned. "We still gotta take her in for the doctors to pronounce her," the taller of the two said.

"I'm US Marshal Slade Brooks, and I'm not releasing her body into your custody. I'll notify the Jackson PD and take it from here."

It wasn't standard procedure, but Duncan could tell the EMTs were buying Slade's story. Federal agents often pulled rank over local law enforcement officials. They shrugged, turned away and headed back to their ambulance.

"The police will be here any minute," Duncan said in a low voice.

It wasn't even a minute before a squad car pulled in. Slade walked outside to chat with the female officer, leaving Duncan to sit beside Chelsey.

He pulled the chair close to the bed. "Stay as still as possible," he whispered.

She didn't answer, and he hoped that she hadn't lost consciousness again. Were they doing the right thing here? Faking her death to help save her life seemed reasonable, but lying didn't come naturally to him and he felt certain the same was true of Chelsey.

The minutes dragged by slowly, but Slade finally returned, bringing Colt with him. "Okay, we're good for now. I've convinced the locals that Chelsey was a federal witness and that we are going to take care of getting her body removed from the hotel."

Duncan stood and pulled the blanket off Chelsey. She blinked up at them. Shifted and winced. Duncan ran a washcloth under cold water and offered it to her. She placed it on the abrasion along the back of her head. "Okay, where are we going?"

"First we need a plan. I don't know that taking the private plane we arranged is the right thing to do, if we're faking Chelsey's death," Slade pointed out. He turned toward Colt. "Did you find anything on the shooter?"

"No, although there was a woman standing off to the side who seemed interested in what was going on. When I went over to talk to her, she took off. She was likely the screamer. I'm fairly certain the guy was set up on the top of the strip mall a few blocks from here." Colt's expression was grim. "They must have narrowed down the two possible locations as this place or the one across the street. The view from the strip mall encompasses both hotels."

"How did they know that?" Chelsey asked. When she tried to sit up, he slid his arm around her shoulders offering his support. She leaned against him just for a moment, and he fought the urge to kiss her.

"I don't know," Colt admitted. "They must have had someone up there watching since early this morning."

"No one is up there now?" Duncan asked.

Colt shook his head. "No, but that doesn't mean they aren't watching from somewhere close by."

"We need to get Chelsey out of here, then." Duncan didn't want to give these guys another chance to get to her. She eased away from him, so he rose to his feet. "Does the plane you arranged for have the ability to have Chelsey lying flat in the back?"

"No, but I can arrange a different plane." Slade pulled out his phone.

"Wait, where are you taking me?" Chelsey asked.

Slade glanced at Duncan. "I'm not sure yet, but I'll figure something out."

"I'm going with her," Duncan said in a firm voice.

"You can't," Chelsey protested weakly.

"She's right, it's too risky," Colt added.

He tamped down a flash of impatience. "First of all, it makes sense that I would go along with her body if she really was dead. Secondly, there's no risk since I'm willing to give up my old life to create a new one with Chelsey."

Colt and Slade exchanged a glance. Duncan was prepared for the argument, but it didn't come.

"Give me a minute to arrange new transportation," Slade said, turning away. "We'll have time to make a plan once I have that arranged."

Duncan let out a breath he hadn't realized he was holding. He smiled reassuringly at Chelsey. "Don't worry, it's going to be all right."

She gave a slight nod, then turned to lie down on the bed.

"Cold?" He drew the blanket up beneath her chin.

She shook her head and closed her eyes. Understanding she needed to rest, he left her alone.

Giving her time to recover from her injuries was one thing, but those moments he'd believed she'd been killed were too fresh in his mind.

No way was he letting her go.

She needed a chance to talk to Slade alone. Ignoring the throbbing pain in her head and chest was easy compared to the impact of Duncan's offer to give up his entire life for her.

She couldn't let him do it.

When Slade returned, she reached out to grasp his hand. In a low whisper she said, "Don't let Duncan give up his family for me."

Slade offered a wry smile. "I'll try, but he's pretty stubborn."

"Please, Slade. You need to find a way." She released his hand and dropped the subject when Duncan came into the room.

"The sooner we get out of here, the better," Duncan said.

"We need to carry Chelsey's body out of the hotel and place her in the back of the SUV," Slade said in agreement. "I recommend we cover her with a sheet, the way we would if she was dead."

"Maybe we use the blanket to carry her out in a sling," Duncan offered. "Use the sheet to cover her face."

It felt odd to hear them talking about how to move her out of the hotel. She hoped Slade and Colt were wrong about the shooter hanging around to keep a watch on the place.

If he were smart, he'd be long gone.

Keeping her body limp as the men lifted her in the blanket wasn't easy. She concentrated on not moving a single muscle.

Duncan and Colt gently set her in the back of the SUV. With part of the back seat lowered flat, she fit perfectly. Only after they closed the hatch did she take a deep breath.

So far, so good.

"Chelsey? The windows are tinted so no one is able to see in. Would you rather sit upright?" Duncan asked.

Her head still hurt, as did her ribs. "No, this is good."

The ride to the airport didn't take long, and she appreciated the way Slade drove with care, staying just under the speed limit.

From her position, she could see the airplanes taking off and landing as they approached the airport. She knew the Jackson Hole Airport was small with just six gates total. But that was for commercial flights. She didn't know where the private hangars were located.

Slade took a turn, then slowly brought the SUV to a stop. "This is it—the private plane we've arranged as transport is waiting inside. We're going to carry you in the blanket, the same way we did at the hotel."

Duncan reached out to lightly stroke her hair in a way that brought tears to her eyes, before pushing his door open. She swiped at her face and reminded herself to stay strong.

Duncan deserved to return to his family.

Once again, she made herself limp, not daring to breathe as she was removed from the SUV. Even when there was a slight bump against the back of her already sore head, she didn't react.

She was carried inside the hangar and placed in the back of a small cargo type of plane. There, she sat up and looked around. This was the first time she'd been in a small plane, and in a private hangar. The interior of the building was rather plain, but also vaguely familiar.

Maybe from something she'd seen on television?

The pilot came over to greet Slade. "I'm Jenkins, your pilot. I need to finish my preflight checklist and we'll be ready to go."

"Thanks. I'm Slade Brooks, and this is Chelsey. We appreciate you changing the plane at the last minute."

Jenkins shrugged. "It's no problem."

"Hey, isn't that building over there the hangar for Travis Wolfe?" Duncan asked.

She craned her neck to see what he

meant. The building was larger than the one they were currently in, but the outside was labeled with a large sign that read Wolfe Industries.

Edging out of the back of the plane, she saw the three men staring in surprise. "We should have realized there would be a private hangar for Travis Wolfe," Duncan said in disgust. "What rich guy doesn't own his own plane?"

"Hey, it's a world outside my experience," Slade commented dryly.

"I need to take a look inside the place," Duncan said. "Could be something there to give us a clue if Travis Wolfe and his head of security, Wesley Strand, are working on the wrong side of the law with Nettles."

Her stomach clenched with worry. "I don't think that's a good idea. What if you get caught?"

"I just need a minute to check the place out." Duncan glanced at Slade. "Don't take off with Chelsey until I'm back, okay?"

It occurred to her that they could leave

while Duncan was off peeking inside the Wolfe Industries hangar. It was the best way to ensure that he didn't try to relocate with her. But Chelsey couldn't do it. She wanted to hug Duncan one last time. She wanted to look into his deep brown eyes and tell him how much these past few days had meant to her.

She wanted to let him know how much she loved him. And would never forget him.

"Duncan, wait," Slade protested, but it was too late. Duncan had already edged out of the hangar, rounded the SUV and was walking purposefully toward the Wolfe Industries building.

"I'll go with him," Colt said. "Stay with Chelsey."

Slade sighed heavily and she knew he was annoyed with Duncan's determination to glimpse inside the building.

From her position in the back of the plane, she watched as Colt and Duncan made their way across the wide-open space that separated the two hangars.

The guys had just reached the edge of the building when a limo rolled into view. She hadn't seen any limos in Jackson and knew the passenger could only be the owner himself. "Slade? What if Travis Wolfe finds them snooping around?"

Slade's expression was grim as he picked up his phone. "Colt? You've got a limo driving up to the hangar."

She couldn't hear Colt's reply, but could only watch in horror as Duncan and Colt dropped down behind a couple of oil drums located right outside the hangar mere seconds before the limo rolled to a stop.

What was Duncan thinking? What if he and Colt were found? It was possible that Travis Wolfe wasn't involved in any criminal activity and would be upset only about the men snooping near his hangar, but she didn't really believe it.

Please, Lord, keep Duncan and Colt safe in Your care!

SIXTEEN

Duncan made himself as small as possible behind the two oil drums located outside the Wolfe Industries hangar. Colt had unexpectedly joined him, and he was glad to have backup. Before taking cover, he'd gotten a glimpse of the interior of the hangar. The space was large, occupied by a plane, but there had also been a slew of boxes along one side of the building, several labeled with the Coyote Creek Construction logo.

As he hovered there behind the oil drum, Duncan slowly realized this was the same place he'd seen in Brett's two photographs of Nettles holding a gun—one photo the gun was pointed at Perry, the other with the undercover cop lying on the floor in a pool of blood.

The shooting of Roland Perry hadn't taken place in a company warehouse, as he'd originally assumed. It had happened right here in the Wolfe Industries airport hangar.

If only there was a way to prove it. The boxes alone wouldn't be enough. But maybe if luminol was used on the interior of the building, they'd find Roland Perry's blood had seeped into the concrete floor. Of course, they needed a warrant and probable cause to get that.

Was the photograph of Nettles and the dead cop standing near Coyote Creek Construction boxes enough? Probably not.

Male voices drifted toward them, and he strained to listen.

"You better hope she's dead," a deep, curt voice said. "I'm tired of paying for incompetence."

She who? Chelsey? Duncan risked a

glance at Colt who was listening just as intently.

"Hey, it's not our fault she managed to get help," a higher whiney voice complained. "We've lost two of our own men in this."

"Shut up!" The deep voice struck with the force of whiplash. "Those men were stupid enough to get caught, so it's only right that they should suffer an *accident* while in jail."

Accident? Duncan's gut clenched. Like being silenced, permanently?

"Easy, Travis..." A third calm voice seemed to be taking the role of peacekeeper.

"No, I won't take it easy," the deep voice snapped. "Why would you guys use hunting rifles anyway? Why not high powered AK47s with silencers attached? This has been nothing but a debacle from the beginning. It's a wonder you were able to hit Thompson the way you did."

The reference to Brett's murder made

Duncan's blood run cold. He peered around the edge of the oil drum just far enough to see four men standing there. He easily recognized three of them from the photos—Anthony Nettles, Wesley Strand and Travis Wolfe. The fourth man was standing apart from the other three, keeping his head down and shoulders slouched as if he were the low man on the totem pole in the group.

The guy with his head down turned so that Duncan could see his profile. *Wait a minute.* Duncan narrowed his gaze, wishing he had a pair of binoculars. The longer he looked, the more convinced he became that the fourth guy was the same one who'd attacked him on the side of the mountain. At least he was fairly certain. Even from a distance he could see the fresh wound along his temple. The spot where Chelsey had hit him with the log during their struggle with the knife.

He eased back behind the drum and glanced at Colt. "They're in it together," he said in a whisper. "The guy with the whiney voice and head down is the same one who attacked me on the mountain."

Colt nodded to indicate he understood.

"A hunting rifle doesn't raise suspicion. Every man in Wyoming has one," the whiney voice said. "But anyone catching a glimpse of a fancy AK47 would blab to the entire town."

"I told you to shut up!" Wolfe sounded as if he had reached his limit.

"Okay, Travis, you have a right to be upset. But the woman is dead and we'll get the property, which is what you wanted, right?"

"Right." Wolfe's tone had lost some of its edge. "I'm getting out of here until things cool off. The rest of you better keep your heads down and eyes open. Those guys who were helping the woman are law enforcement of some kind and might stick around to find out what happened to her."

"Not to worry, we have inside help, remember?" The nasal voice must belong to

Nettles, it was the first thing the guy had said since they'd arrived.

"Yes, inside help that I'm paying for," Wolfe responded harshly. "I'm funding all of this, so you guys better hold up your end of the deal."

Duncan realized this was exactly what they needed to nail these guys once and for all. Easing his phone out of his pocket, he held it along the edge of the oil drum, much the way Brett must have done a few weeks ago, and took pictures of the four men standing outside the hangar.

The only downside he could see was that he and Colt might be trespassing, although he felt certain the hangar itself might belong to the airport. Still, it was something that could get their testimony tossed out of a courtroom by a smart lawyer, one he assumed Wolfe had on speed dial.

He thought about the boxes inside the hangar and wondered what Coyote Creek Construction was shipping in or out of the state of Wyoming.

They needed something, anything to use as probable cause to search the place.

But what?

"What did you do with the hunting rifle, Stewart?" the calm voice asked.

"I—uh, still have it," whiney voice replied. "But I can get rid of it if you'd like."

"Why would you keep it?" Wolfe's tone was incredulous. "How incompetent are you?"

The sound of a fist striking skin followed by a muffled thud reached his ears. Duncan risked another glance around the drum to see someone lying on the concrete. Stewart, aka whiney voice.

One of the three men in charge had hit the underling hard enough to knock him unconscious.

And if he and Colt didn't do something, then there was nothing to stop them from killing him.

"Get rid of him," Wolfe said tersely. "I'm done here. Call me when you manage to get everything under control."

Duncan tensed. Wolfe was going to get on his personal plane and get out of Wyoming unless they found a way to keep him there.

But how?

There was a scuffle as Stewart was picked up off the ground and tossed in the back of the limo. Duncan risked another glance around the oil drum and couldn't see Travis Wolfe anywhere. He must have gone deeper into the hangar.

The other two men slid into the back of the limo as ordered. He eased back and glanced at Colt. "You take the limo, I'll try to delay the plane."

"How are you going to do that?"

Duncan shook his head because he didn't have an answer. All he knew was that if Wolfe took off, then their chances of getting him in custody dropped significantly.

Duncan took a deep breath and lunged from behind the oil drums. Without hesitation, he darted inside the hangar as the plane began to roll past.

Without thinking, he grabbed onto one of the wings, as if his weight would be enough to stop it.

But of course, it wasn't.

Someone from the limo must have noticed him dangling from the wing of the plane like a broken hood ornament because he heard someone yell out, "Hey! That's the guy who's been protecting the woman!"

He couldn't hear anything beyond the roar of the airplane engines as the plane gained speed. He mentally braced himself, expecting at any moment to feel the searing pain from a bullet.

Chelsey watched the drama unfold with disbelief. What was Duncan doing hanging from the plane?

In some part of her mind she heard Slade calling the police even though they had no idea who within the department they could trust. She jumped down from the back of the cargo plane, the jarring movement causing her head and ribs to protest with pain.

It wasn't easy to catch her breath, but she didn't care. She sprinted out of the hangar toward the limo that had come to an abrupt stop.

"What in the—she's alive?" someone shouted incredulously.

She'd blown her cover of pretending to be dead, but it didn't matter.

Not if Duncan died for real.

As if he'd heard her thoughts, he abruptly let go of the plane, falling and landing in a heap on the tarmac. Something whizzed past her head and after a few seconds it registered in a corner of her brain that one of the men from the limo was shooting at her.

Again.

"Get down," Slade roared, grabbing her from behind.

She fell forward onto her hands and

knees as Slade placed himself in front of her. Slade fired at the limo, shattering one of the windows. From where she was, she could see several things happening at once.

Colt stood and took aim, firing at the plane. Smoke billowed out from behind the aircraft, and it lurched to one side. She watched in horror as the plane crookedly descended back down to the runway.

Duncan ran toward the limo with his gun in his hand. "Police! Drop your weapons, now!"

Slade leveled his weapon. "US Marshals Service! Toss your guns down or we will shoot."

When Colt turned, the men in the limo realized they were outnumbered. Even if they got a couple of shots off, one or more of them would die.

"Okay, okay!" Nettles caved first, tossing his gun down to the ground.

"Kick it away," Duncan demanded.

Nettles did as he was told. Wesley

Strand followed suit, tossing his weapon down and kicking it aside as well.

"Slade, take over for me. I'm going after Wolfe." Duncan turned and headed back toward the plane that was now lopsided on the ground, like a wounded bird.

"Duncan, no! Come back!" She shouted as loud as possible, but he never hesitated, sprinting toward the plane.

"Where's the other guy?" Slade asked, ignoring her plea. "The one Wolfe hit in the head."

"Back there." Nettles jerked his thumb toward the inside of the limo.

"Cover them, Colt," Slade said. "I need to see if he's alive."

Chelsey pushed herself upright, her gaze following Duncan's form as he closed the distance to the plane. After seeing how callously Wolfe had struck one of the men, sending him crashing to the ground, she knew the millionaire wouldn't hesitate to do the same to Duncan.

Or worse.

* * *

Duncan held his gun in a two-handed grip as he approached the plane. No surprise that the bird sat there, without anyone coming out from the aircraft.

"Wolfe, I know you're in there," Duncan called, pressing his back against the plane. "We've got your cohorts in custody, so you may as well give yourself up."

No response from the plane occupants. Duncan knew this wouldn't be easy. The rich guy inside was accustomed to getting his way.

"Wolfe, the feds are putting you under arrest for assault and battery," Duncan continued. "Come out with your hands up where I can see them."

Still nothing. He wished he could hear what the conversation was inside the plane. Was Travis Wolfe trying to find a way to get out of here? There was plenty of wide-open space on the runway, but nothing could be done to fix the damaged plane.

Or did the millionaire know that Duncan didn't have jurisdiction here in Jackson, Wyoming? He wished he'd thought of asking the US Marshals to deputize him.

The door cracked open. "Don't shoot— I'm coming out." Wolfe's voice didn't sound as curt as it had before, but Duncan didn't think the guy was going to give up so easily.

One long leg came out, then the other. The guy jumped to the ground, then spun toward Duncan. In a nanosecond, Duncan saw the gun in his hand and pulled the trigger of his weapon.

The one that had once belonged to the guy Wolfe had struck to the ground.

Duncan ducked but there was no need as the bullet from Wolfe's gun went wide. Then a shout of rage erupted from Wolfe.

"You shot me!" Wolfe looked shocked that anyone had dared to do such a thing. But the gun he held in his right arm was pointing to the ground now as blood dripped from a wound in his upper right arm.

The arm holding the weapon.

"Put the gun down!" Duncan repeated. "Or I'll shoot again."

Wolfe dropped the weapon and then reached up to cover his wound. "I'll have your badge for this. You shot an innocent man!"

Duncan edged closer until he was able to put his foot on the gun and sweep it beneath the plane. Then he came closer still, looking Wolfe right in the eye.

"The feds are right here, and you're under arrest for assault and conspiracy to commit murder," Duncan said. "You have the right to remain silent. Anything you say can and will be used against you in a court of law." He was about to continue the Miranda warning when he caught movement from the corner of his eye from inside the plane.

Glancing over, he saw the pilot was holding a gun, the muzzle pointed directly at him. Duncan froze.

"Shoot him!" Wolfe screamed. "What are you waiting for? Shoot him!"

The pilot stared at him, and Duncan refused to look away. If the guy was going to shoot, he wanted to see it in his eyes.

But the pilot looked uncertain. Duncan suspected the guy had never shot at anyone before—and hoped and prayed that he wouldn't do so now.

Stalemate.

Long seconds ticked by, and he believed the pilot couldn't do it. Dragging his gaze back to Wolfe, Duncan shugged. "Guess that's not part of the plan, Wolfe."

"I pay you to do as I say!" Wolfe hissed at the pilot.

In response, the pilot dropped the gun and placed his hands in the air. "I'm not a part of this."

"Seems killing a man crosses the line." Duncan gestured at Wolfe with the gun. "Turn around and put your hands up against the plane."

"Duncan!" Chelsey's voice rang out

from behind him, but he didn't dare take his gaze off Wolfe.

The millionaire's eyes widened comically. "What? She's alive?"

For the first time in what seemed like forever, Duncan smiled. "Yes, she is. And you're going away for a long time."

"I don't think so," Wolfe sneered. "My lawyers will get me out of this mess."

Duncan knew his threat wasn't an idle one. Money talked and the rich often found a way to get out of tight spots. Witnesses were paid off and recanted their stories, for starters.

But not this time. He wasn't going to recant his testimony and neither would Chelsey.

The US Marshals were witnesses, too.

Wolfe finally turned and put his hands up against the plane. Duncan didn't have a set of handcuffs on him, so he glanced at Chelsey.

"See if you can find something to tie him up with," he told her.

Her wide eyes locked on his before she nodded. Before she could head over to Colt and Slade, the pilot tossed out some rope.

"Use this," he said in a resigned tone. "I should have known this job was too good to be true. The guy pays well, but he's a massive jerk."

"Thanks." Duncan eyed the pilot carefully as he picked up the rope, just in case this was some sort of trick.

"Chelsey, hold the gun on him, will you? And if he moves, shoot."

Chelsey took the gun, holding it with both hands that indicated to him that this wasn't the first time.

The pilot jumped to the ground, and there was no sign of the gun. Duncan used the rope to tie Wolfe's wrists together.

"That hurts," Wolfe complained. "You shot me, remember?"

"Yeah, because you shot at me, first, remember?" Duncan shook his head in disgust. "Your pilot is a witness."

The pilot lifted his hands. "Hey, I didn't really see anything," he protested. "I'm hired to fly the plane where Mr. Wolfe wants me to, nothing more."

Great, just great. Wolfe's lawyers would surely find a way to turn this around on him, but he couldn't worry about that now.

"Duncan? Need help?" Colt jogged over. "We have the other two cuffed, and the guy in the back of the limo is still out cold."

"We should notify the local police," Duncan said.

"Already done. They'll be here any moment. Can't you hear the sirens?"

Duncan turned and saw that indeed two police cars were barreling toward them with lights flashing and sirens wailing. He knew Wolfe had an inside man, but it wasn't likely both sets of officers were involved in this.

It was over. He took a step toward Chelsey and she threw her arms around his neck, hanging on as if her life depended on it.

"I was so scared," she whispered.

"I know. Me, too." He clutched her close, then drew back enough to look into her blue eyes. Then, realizing it might be the last time he'd have the chance, he lowered his mouth and kissed her.

She melted against him, but he couldn't allow himself to read too much into her actions.

Gratitude and friendship weren't love.

And he couldn't allow his heart to be broken a second time.

SEVENTEEN

Chelsey reveled in Duncan's sweet kiss, holding him tightly and unwilling to let him go. His kiss held a note of desperation that matched hers, and she knew they were both thinking along the same lines. That this was it.

The last time they'd see each other.

"Chelsey." Her name was a mere whisper as he lifted his head, and she ached with longing. In the moment she'd watched Duncan hanging from the plane, she'd realized just how much she loved him.

With a depth that wasn't a fraction of what she'd felt for Brett. But this wasn't the time to relive her previous mistakes.

"Duncan, I'm so glad you're safe." She blinked tears from her eyes, gazing up at him and memorizing the moment. It was all she'd have to remember him by once she was gone.

"You shouldn't have come out of hiding, Chelsey." His tone was gentle, but she saw the worry in his dark gaze. "Now these guys know you're still alive."

"Yes, but we have them all in custody anyway, right? So does it really matter? They'll all go to jail for this, won't they?"

He hesitated in a way that sent a frisson of alarm skittering through her. "You have to know that Wolfe is going to hire heavy hitter lawyers. If there's a way to get him off, they'll find it."

"But we have a lot of witnesses on our side." Chelsey didn't want to believe any of these men would get away with what they'd done. Killing Roland Perry, an undercover cop, then going on to murder Brett. Coming after her and Duncan, and finally shooting her outside the hotel.

Surely, they'd pay for their crimes.

God wouldn't let any of them, even Wolfe, simply walk away, would He?

Police sirens grew louder, and she noticed Duncan looking over her shoulder. Reluctantly releasing him, she turned to watch two police cars driving up to the Wolfe Industries hangar.

Duncan shifted so that he was standing in front of her. She frowned, then remembered they weren't entirely sure who to trust within the Jackson Police Department. Still, she didn't think it was likely a dirty cop would try something here with all these people around.

Including two federal marshals.

"Let's head back to the private hangar where the cargo plane is located," Duncan murmured in a low voice.

"I'm sure we're not going to be leaving anytime soon," she pointed out.

"Maybe not, but humor me anyway. It doesn't hurt to have a possible escape route in case things go sideways." Duncan moved toward the hangar.

Go sideways? She didn't like the sound of that. Still, she decided there was no reason to argue.

Four police officers had emerged from the two squad cars, coming over to talk to Colt and Slade. The three bound men had been shoved into the back of the limo. She frowned, wondering if the driver had remained behind the wheel.

As if hearing her thoughts, Colt opened the driver's side door and motioned with his gun for the driver to get out. She breathed a sigh of relief.

"Duncan, do you think that once we testify against these guys we can go back to our normal lives?"

He glanced at her, remaining silent until they'd reached the cargo plane. "Honestly, I don't know, Chelsey. If these guys are the main players, then maybe. But you have to understand the wheels of justice don't move fast. And with Wolfe's high-priced legal team, I wouldn't be surprised if this dragged on for years."

"Years?" The tiny flame of hope withered and died.

"Hey, we're going to be okay." Duncan smiled. "I'll be with you the entire time."

"Wait, what? You can't give up your family for me, Duncan. That's too great a sacrifice."

"After what I've witnessed here, I don't think there's any other option," he countered, his expression turning serious. "I heard them talk about how glad they were you were dead, Chelsey. And they mentioned Brett's murder, too. I'm just as much a part of this case as you are."

She stared at him for a long moment, knowing he was right, yet wishing he was wrong. "Even so, that doesn't mean we'd be relocated together. In fact, it would be more likely that the federal marshal program would insist we be separated."

His brow furrowed. "That's not happening. We're sticking together, Chelsey. You have my word."

"But… I don't want you to feel obligated

to stay with me." It wasn't easy to put her feelings into words. "You have a family to return to when the trial is over."

Duncan's dark brown gaze bored into hers but before he could respond, Slade crossed over.

"The police want us to go to the station to provide statements about what transpired here." Slade glanced over his shoulder, then added, "I don't love the idea since we still don't know who to trust within the department."

"I know. Wolfe in particular mentioned how he was paying for the guy on the inside who might help them." Duncan gestured with his hand. "Colt heard it, too."

Slade gave a grim nod. "My plan is to have me and Colt go with the cops and the prisoners to the station together to make sure they don't escape. But that leaves you and Chelsey to get there on your own."

There was a moment of silence as Duncan considered Slade's offer.

"I feel safe with Duncan," she offered, in case there was any doubt.

"Okay, but we'll have to get a rental car. You guys should take the SUV," Duncan said.

"No, I think you and Chelsey need it more than we do," Slade protested. "We've requested a police transport van. The limo will remain here until it can be processed."

She glanced at the limo curiously. "You mean they'll look for evidence?"

Slade nodded. "Exactly."

"They need to look at the plane, too," Duncan said. "And they need to wash the inside of Wolfe's hangar with lumi-nol. I'm convinced the murder of Roland Perry took place there. Brett's photos don't show enough of the building, but the photographs along with finding blood evidence should be enough to put Nettles away for a long time."

"Maybe he'll roll over on Travis Wolfe,"

Slade mused. "I'd think he'd be anxious to try to make a deal for a lighter sentence."

"A lighter sentence for murder?" Chelsey couldn't believe what she was hearing.

"Don't worry, he'll spend plenty of time in jail," Slade assured her.

"Looks like the police transport van is on its way," Duncan said, jutting his chin toward the road. "It should be here shortly."

"Take the SUV." Slade lightly tossed the key fob in the air. Duncan easily caught it. "We'll see you down at the station."

Chelsey watched as Slade made his way back to the group of law enforcement officers. The SUV wasn't far, and once the transport van arrived, Duncan cupped her elbow in his hand and nudged her forward.

"Let's go."

She nodded, glancing back at the cargo plane before sliding into the SUV's passenger seat. For a moment, she wanted more than anything to ask the pilot to whisk her and Duncan far away from there, but then a flash of shame followed.

She wouldn't be a coward, slinking away from this. If she needed to testify, she would.

Even if that meant losing everything—especially, and most importantly, Duncan.

Duncan kept an eye on the rearview mirror, watching the group of five men, the original four plus the pilot, being ushered into the police van. They grew distant as he pushed the accelerator to the floor.

In theory, the worst was over. They had the three main men in custody and felt certain they'd stay there, even if they had a cop on their payroll.

He had to physically unclench his fingers from the steering wheel in an attempt to relax his grip. For some reason, he couldn't relax. Couldn't find a way to believe the horror of Brett's murder and that of Roland Perry was over.

There was no reason to be paranoid, but he kept a keen gaze on the traffic behind them as they left the Jackson airport. He wanted to be ready to react, just in case.

So far, so good. He turned off the highway and headed through town to the local police station.

From what seemed like nowhere, a squad car pulled up behind them, red and blue lights flashing. The driver of the squad car also hit the siren, indicating Duncan should stop.

"Why is he pulling us over?" Chelsey asked, worry in her tone. "We didn't break any traffic laws, did we?"

"No." Duncan's gut instincts were screaming at him. Instead of pulling over, he wrenched the steering wheel to the left, and hit the gas. The SUV responded well, barely screeching as he took a hard left.

"What are you doing?" Chelsey gripped the armrest between them. "We can't outrun a cop!"

"Keep an eye on him," Duncan ordered,

as he took more turns in an attempt to shake the squad car off his tail. Not as easy to do in downtown Jackson, a place he wasn't familiar with.

A city the cop behind him could navigate blindfolded.

Chelsey twisted in her seat. "I don't understand. Shouldn't we at least talk to him?"

"Not if he's the one being paid to help get rid of us." Duncan raked his gaze over the area, hoping, praying for some way to escape the cop sticking behind him like a pesky gnat.

Then another squad car materialized from the right, cutting directly in front of him. Duncan had little choice but to yank the SUV over and hit the brake hard, to avoid the inevitable collision.

"Be ready to run," he said in a low, urgent voice.

"No, I'm not leaving you," she whispered.

He didn't like it and reached for his

gun, but a second too late. The officer was already at his driver's side window, his weapon pointed at Duncan.

"Put your hands in the air! Don't touch the gun!"

"I won't!" The last thing Duncan needed was for this guy to be trigger happy.

"Get out of the car with your hands up!"

"Don't shoot! I'm surrendering!" Duncan did as ordered while trying desperately to think of a way out of this mess. He didn't trust either of these guys, but the cop behind him less so than the younger officer holding him at gunpoint.

Holding his hands up high, he kicked the door open. The young officer had taken several steps back, so the abrupt opening of the door didn't come close to touching him. "My name is Duncan O'Hare and I'm a cop with the Milwaukee Police Department."

"Turn around very slowly and put your hands on the top of the vehicle." The officer acted as if he didn't care that Duncan was a fellow cop.

"Thanks JT, I'll take it from here," a voice drawled from behind him.

"Are you sure, Lieutenant?" The officer's tone was respectful but held a distinct note of doubt. "I think it would be better to stay and back you up, just in case they try to make a run for it, again."

"Go ahead and cuff him and the woman," the lieutenant responded. "Then I'll take over."

Duncan shot a quick glance over his shoulder, eyeing the lieutenant. His name tag identified him as Goldberg. He was a big burly guy, with a gut that hung over his belt, and the coldness in his gaze made Duncan suspect this was the guy on Wolfe's payroll.

Not any low-ranking officer, but a lieutenant. He supposed it could be worse—at least the mole wasn't the chief of police.

Unless there were more than one of them on the inside. Not a happy thought.

"Don't leave us with Goldberg," Duncan said in a low, urgent voice, as the young officer slapped a silver bracelet around his right wrist and yanked it down behind his back. "He can't be trusted. If you leave us alone, he'll kill us."

His words fell on deaf ears. The officer brought his left wrist back and finished the job of securing his wrists together. "Hey, Lou, what's the story with these two? They rob a bank or what?"

"Something like that," the lieutenant drawled. "Thanks again for your quick response, JT. You go on, now, and I'll make sure to put a good word in for you."

"Thanks, Lou," the young man responded. Duncan turned so that his cuffed wrists were up against the SUV. He wished Chelsey would have run away. The lieutenant probably wouldn't have been able to catch her, but instead she'd stayed and allowed young JT to place her in cuffs, too. She huddled next to him. He wanted nothing more than to pull her into his arms.

"You sure you don't need anything else?" JT asked. Duncan tried to catch the young officer's gaze—the guy had to realize this was not normal protocol.

Lieutenants rarely came out of their offices to make arrests on the street. Not even in a small town like Jackson, Wyoming, would something like that be a common occurrence.

"JT, you might want to mention this to the federal marshals at the police station," Duncan said quickly. "Slade Brooks and Colt Nelson."

"Marshals?" The young officer hesitated, glancing back at his lieutenant. "You know about that, Lou?"

"I do, and don't let these two innocent faces fool you," he drawled. "They're both wanted for murdering a cop."

"Cops killing cops," JT said in disgust. "Nothin' worse than that."

"You're right," Duncan agreed. "Just ask

your lieutenant, after all his loyalty has been bought and paid for."

The lieutenant moved quickly, pulling his baton and whacking it hard against Duncan's midsection.

The force of the blow had him doubling over, pain shooting through him and the contents of his stomach threatening to erupt. Blackness hovered along the edge of his vision as he tried desperately not to lose consciousness.

"No! Stop it! Please, don't hurt him!" Chelsey's horrified tone helped keep him on his feet.

He would not fall to his knees in front of Lieutenant Goldberg.

"Hey, Lou?" There was an uncertainty to JT's voice that gave Duncan hope.

"I'll take it from here," Goldberg repeated. "Call a tow truck for their SUV, then get back to work." When JT hesitated, he added, "JT? That's a direct order, son."

For second Duncan thought the young

cop might continue arguing, but he didn't. Instead, he turned and made his way back to his squad car. JT opened the driver's side door and slid in behind the wheel.

He backed up, then drove off without giving them a second glance.

Duncan tried to keep his breathing even, despite the throbbing pain. "So now what, Lou?" he asked, mimicking JT's nickname. "Where are you going to take us?"

"Start walking." The lieutenant looked irritated as he lightly tapped the baton against the palm of his hand. Duncan had a sneaking suspicion the man liked hurting others and feared that his next target might be Chelsey.

He couldn't let that happen.

"Okay, you've got us under your control," Duncan agreed. He glanced at Chelsey, using his gaze to indicate she should go ahead of him. "We're not going to cause you any trouble."

"You've already caused me a great deal of trouble," the lieutenant hissed. He moved forward, opened the back seat of his squad car and used the baton to point at the back seat. "Get in."

Duncan swept a glance over the area, hoping to catch the eye of someone, anyone nearby. But the bystanders stayed far back, as if in fear for their lives. Then another squad car sitting at a gas station caught his eye. He stared hard, hoping the driver of the vehicle would take notice. But the car was too far away for him to make a connection.

Chelsey slid in first, moving awkwardly with her hands cuffed behind her back. He tried to give her a reassuring smile, but her pale features were a clear indication of her bone-deep fear.

He wasn't thrilled with the situation, either. But he felt certain the lieutenant would have to think this through. After all, JT knew about the two of them being in his custody. The lieutenant couldn't just shoot them and dump their bodies off in the forest somewhere.

Could he?

He slid in beside Chelsey, the interior of the vehicle stifling hot as the sun beat down through the windows. The lieutenant slammed the door and got in behind the wheel.

Goldberg didn't say anything as he eased into traffic, leaving their SUV behind.

Chelsey was squirming in her seat next to him. "You okay?" he whispered.

She nodded but didn't stop moving around. After a long moment she pulled one arm from around her back, gently brushing against his arm with her hand.

He didn't change his facial expression, even though he was secretly thrilled she'd managed to get one of her hands free of the cuffs. JT hadn't cuffed her hands as tightly as his, a rookie mistake.

Chelsey's being free didn't help much. Without a weapon, or his hands being free, their ability to escape the burly lieutenant unscathed was not looking good.

EIGHTEEN

Chelsey kept her hands low, so that the big cop wouldn't notice she'd managed to get one wrist free.

Not that being uncuffed was much help. What could they do from the back of a squad car? Especially when the doors couldn't be opened from the inside.

"I told you to run," Duncan whispered.

She ignored him. Running and leaving him behind wasn't an option. If this was going to end—she swallowed hard—then so be it. She chose to believe in God's plan, and maybe being here with Duncan would make it easier for both of them.

Remembering the bobby pins in her hair, she lowered her head, and eased her left wrist up high enough to pull two from her curls. Was it possible they could use them to unlock Duncan's cuffs?

Without saying anything, she pressed the bobby pins against his hand so he'd know she had them. He didn't so much as glance at her, keeping his gaze on the cop behind the wheel, but he shifted just enough that she could access the cuffs.

Still, it was an impossible task considering she couldn't see what she was doing and needed to make it seem as if her wrists were still together. Thankfully, for whatever reason, the lieutenant didn't look at them, his attention focused on the road.

Was he right now trying to find a place to silence the two of them forever?

Chelsey swallowed hard and prayed that God would give her and Duncan the strength and courage they needed to get through this.

The squad car slowed and the lieutenant pulled off the main thoroughfare onto a winding dirt road. Chelsey tensed, sensing this was not good.

"Where are you taking us?" Duncan asked. "Shouldn't you be taking two people suspected for killing a cop to the precinct to be booked?"

"Shut up," Goldberg growled.

Duncan shifted again, giving her better access to his cuffed wrists. She realized his conversation was a diversion from her attempt to free him.

"I wasn't kidding about the federal marshals," Duncan said. "When we end up missing and/or dead, they're going to know someone within the police department was involved. Even the not-so-bright JT will put two and two together to come up with four."

The lieutenant didn't respond. The squad car jostled side to side as the road grew more uneven. Chelsey bumped against Duncan, still working the bobby pin in the keyhole of the handcuffs.

Somehow, the rocking motion of the squad car along with her efforts caused the lock to spring open. She wanted to smile and shout with joy when Duncan's wrists came apart but managed to keep her expression impassive.

A minor victory, because they weren't out of this mess, not by a mile. The cop was armed and they weren't.

"Travis Wolfe is going to throw you under the bus," Duncan said as he gently took the bobby pin from her fingers. "You know very well he'll do whatever is necessary to save his own skin. Millionaires are not cut out for prison. Killing us isn't going to stop the avalanche of evidence the feds have against him. In fact, if you were smart, you'd take the money you've squirreled away and get out of town before anyone else realizes you've been working for him."

"I said shut up!" The sudden shout from the lieutenant startled her so badly, she was glad she didn't have the bobby pins, or she'd have dropped them. Risking a glance down to his hands, she could see that Duncan still had the two bobby pins, straightened into thin spears.

Hardly a lethal weapon, but better than nothing.

"Okay, fine, have it your way." Duncan glanced over with a grim expression. She could tell there was a lot he wanted to say but couldn't.

She felt the same way.

The squad car jerked to an abrupt halt. She tensed, then quickly followed Duncan's lead by placing her hands behind her back in an effort to hide the fact she was free.

The large man climbed out of the squad car and opened Duncan's door. "Get out."

Duncan turned in his seat, swinging his legs out of the car. As he braced himself to stand, she heard the sound of a car engine.

From there, things happened fast. The lieutenant glanced over to see who was driving on the road as Duncan launched himself from the squad car, shoving at the cop with his unbound wrists, the bobby pin stabbing near the lieutenant's eye.

The big cop screamed in pain and the sound of a gunshot made her ears ring. She scrambled out of the vehicle after Duncan, frantically looking for something she could use as a weapon against the cop. There was a rock near the edge of the vehicle and she quickly bent down and scooped it up.

Duncan and the cop were struggling for the gun, the blunt end pointed upward. It was reminiscent of the struggle Duncan had with the assailant on the mountain that first night.

The engine noise grew louder. Chelsey wasn't going to wait. Darting around the two men, she brought the rock down on the back of the lieutenant's head.

Again, the big man howled in pain and it proved to be enough of a distraction for Duncan to wrench the gun free. But somehow, the gun went off during the struggle. It took her a minute to verify Duncan hadn't been hit.

With a blood-curdling scream, the man went down, clutching his wounded arm. "I'll kill you for this!"

"Chelsey? We have to go." The words barely left his mouth when another Jackson PD squad car pulled up, a female officer swiftly jumping from the vehicle, her gun pointed at them.

"Put your hands in the air where I can see them!" she shouted.

The lieutenant managed to stop his screaming long enough to register what was happening. "Kimball, shoot them! They're trying to escape!"

"You know that's not true," Duncan responded in a low, even tone. "You saw him take custody of us back in downtown Jackson, didn't you? You were in the squad car parked in the gas station."

Officer Kimball didn't answer and stayed where she was, her weapon trained on them.

"You have to ask yourself why your boss would bring us here rather than down to the police station," Duncan continued. "It's because he intended to kill us to prevent us from telling everyone the truth about the bribe money he's taken over the years from Travis Wolfe."

Officer Kimball's gaze flickered to the lieutenant then returned to Duncan. "Put the gun down."

"I can't do that, not until your boss is neutralized." Duncan held his hands up so the weapon in his hand wasn't a threat. "He won't hesitate to kill you, too."

Chelsey stepped forward, her gaze pleading with the female cop, who was roughly her own age, to believe them. "I'm Chelsey Robards, the owner of the Teton Valley Hotel, and I've been on the run since my fiancé was shot at our wedding. I know you'll find this difficult to believe, but your boss really did intend to kill us. Because we know the truth."

Kimball hesitated, then gave a short jerk

of her head. "Okay, back away from the lieutenant and keep the gun where I can see it. If you make a move toward me, I will shoot first and ask questions later."

"You…believe us?" Chelsey asked as she and Duncan took several steps far away from the lieutenant.

"I was under the impression you were dead, Chelsey. At least, that's what the federal marshals told me at the hotel." Officer Kimball's tone was wry. "I'd rather get everyone down to the police station to sort this out."

"Can't you see these two shot me?" the lieutenant raged. "I'll have your badge for taking their word over mine."

"I don't think so, Lou." Kimball's tone held a bit of snark that Chelsey appreciated. "I followed you here, remember? And I can't think of a good reason for you to have brought two suspects to this remote location unless it was to get rid of them. Now shut up while I call for backup. Preferably anyone other than JT."

A wave of relief washed over her. Chelsey leaned against Duncan, her knees weak.

Officer Kimball believed them.

It was over.

Duncan didn't like being separated from Chelsey. As a cop he knew the importance of interviewing key witnesses separately, but he didn't like not having her close.

He loved her. As much as he'd tried not to, he'd fallen deeply in love with Chelsey. And when this was over, he wanted to be with her. No matter where, or what names they'd have or what they'd be doing for work.

His life wasn't worth living without Chelsey.

Yet he wasn't entirely sure she felt the same way about him, considering she'd refused his offer to go into WITSEC with her more than once.

He decided to try to put his worry into God's hands, knowing He had a plan for them. Hopefully, a plan that included the two of them being together.

He'd told the story of Lieutenant Goldberg taking him and Chelsey away at gunpoint and driving them to the dirt road and abandoned building several times now. He admitted the gun had gone off in the struggle, injuring the lieutenant. Yet he knew the drill. Any cop being shot in the line of duty was a big deal and this was no exception.

He imagined Chelsey had told the same story several times as well. Hopefully they'd let her go by now, since he was the one who'd accidentally used the lieutenant's gun against him.

And where were the feds? Did Slade and Colt have Wolfe, Nettles and Strand locked up in the same cell or had they been separated, too?

How many jail cells did Jackson have anyway?

The door to his interview room opened and Slade Brooks walked in. Duncan managed a weary grin. "About time you showed up."

"It took longer than it should to get the police chief to believe Goldberg was really a dirty cop," Slade admitted, dropping into the chair across from him. "Colt managed to dig deep enough to find recent phone calls between Strand and Goldberg, so that helped. Once we find the money Goldberg has stashed away, we'll have everything we need."

"Officer Kimball tell you what happened?" Duncan asked.

Slade nodded. "Yes, Officer Kimball told me exactly what she'd witnessed both in Jackson and again out on the dirt road." Slade shrugged. "It helped that I'd spoken to her after we decided to fake Chelsey's death. She remembered me and Colt and was smart enough to figure out the rest."

"If she hadn't arrived when she did, we'd be dead," Duncan said. "All I had to defend myself was a couple of bobby pins Chelsey used to unlock the cuffs."

"I don't know. I think you'd have found a way," Slade drawled.

The backhanded compliment drew a reluctant grin. "Thanks for the vote of confidence."

Slade glanced at the door. "The cops picked up Kenny Martin as he arrived at the airport hangar, and he's already talking about cutting a deal. And I think once Stewart regains consciousness, he'll add his two cents."

"Good. Sounds like you'll have everything tied up in a nice bow."

"That's the plan." Slade hesitated, then added, "They're letting you go for now, but both the federal marshals and the local police will need you to testify against Nettles, Wolfe and Strand."

"I know." Duncan cleared his throat. "What about Chelsey?"

Slade considered him for a moment. "Fact is, Chelsey doesn't really have as much evidence to provide compared to you, Duncan. We have Brett's photographs, and both you and Colt heard Wolfe, Nettles and Strand talk about killing Brett and attempting to kill Chelsey. She doesn't have anything additional to offer, other than to corroborate what we already know."

Duncan straightened in his seat. "What are you saying, Slade? I'm the one that needs to go into WITSEC instead of Chelsey?"

Slade spread his hands wide. "The main reason we offered WITSEC to Brett Thompson was because he was a witness to a murder and we believed the death was related to organized crime. Now it's looking more like Wolfe is the brains behind everything. He got greedy, the boxes in the airport hanger contain drugs, which is what Kenny Martin had come to pick up, and of course we know Wolfe wanted the land. But other than that, we haven't found any true organized crime ring. With Wolfe and the others in custody, I'm not sure WITSEC is really necessary for either of you."

"Not necessary?" Duncan frowned. "I'd rather Chelsey be safe."

Slade shrugged. "We can certainly provide new identities for you both, if that's what you'd prefer."

Once again, Duncan thought about his dad, Ian O'Hare, his sister, Shayla Callahan, his brother-in-law, Mike Callahan, and the other Callahans.

Plus his nephew, Brodie, and niece, Breena.

He would miss his family very much. But there was no way on earth he could live without Chelsey. "I want Chelsey to be safe," he repeated. "Whatever it takes. And her staying here in Wyoming doesn't seem reasonable."

"Okay, we'll put some things in motion." Slade stood and crossed over to the door. Then he paused and glanced back over his shoulder. "I did a little research on you, Duncan. Not only are you a cop, your dad is a retired cop, and your sister married into a family full of law enforcement types. If you ask me, there isn't a safer place for you and Chelsey than with them. After all, Milwaukee is pretty far from Jackson, Wyoming." Slade opened the door and left.

Leaving Duncan to absorb the impact of his words.

Was Slade right? If there weren't any true organized crime members to come after them, was it really necessary for him and Chelsey to disappear forever?

Or was this nothing more than wishful thinking on his part?

The door opened again and this time, Chelsey stepped in. He rose to meet her halfway, stunned when she launched herself into his arms.

"Oh, Duncan, that took forever. I couldn't wait to see you."

He nestled her close, lowering his cheek to her hair. "I'm okay, Chels. How are you?"

"Fine now," was her muffled reply. She wound her arms around his waist and hung on as if she'd never let go.

He didn't mind. If he had his way, he'd never let her go, either.

"I love you, Chelsey." He'd promised himself if they got away from Goldberg alive, he'd tell her how he felt. "I know you probably don't feel the same way, and I know you don't want to mistake friendship for love, but it's important to me that you know the truth."

"Duncan." Her voice was so low he could barely hear it. She hesitated, then lifted her face to his. Tears shimmered in her eyes. "I love you, too, and I realized my feelings for Brett weren't the real thing because I was attracted to you from the start. I've fallen in love with you, but I can't ask you to give up your family for me."

"Really?" He searched her gaze, afraid to hope. "Slade told me that I'm the one who is more at risk as far as needing to testify against these guys, Chelsey. So if anything it would be me needing the protection of being in WITSEC, not you."

Her brow furrowed. "Slade said that?"

The tiny flicker of hope in his heart went out. "Yes, but even so, Chelsey, I don't think staying in Wyoming is in your best interest. I thought it might be better for you to relocate to Milwaukee, the place where you once lived with your parents. My family will look after you for me."

"And where will you be, Duncan?"

He longed to kiss her, but forced himself to do what was best for her. "I plan to trust God's plan for us. And if that means me disappearing, while you stay safe with my family, then I'll gladly take that. Anything is possible as long as I know you're safe."

Her blue eyes softened. "And what if I want to be with you?"

His heart stuttered in his chest. "I'd like nothing more, but I need you to be sure, Chelsey. This is a big step with some level of risk involved."

There was a series of shouts and cries from outside the interview room. Duncan reacted by spinning Chelsey away from the door and placing himself in front of her, ready to fight if necessary.

The minutes ticked by slowly, then Slade poked his head inside. "You both okay?"

Duncan gave a curt nod. "What happened?"

"Fight broke out in the jail cell. Wolfe lost his temper and attacked Strand." Slade sighed. "Strand won that fight, but Wolfe has died of his injuries. Looks like the only one you have to testify against is Strand, who doesn't have nearly the same high-powered attorneys Wolfe had access to." The marshal grinned wryly. "Our job just got a whole lot easier."

The news swirled in his head. "You really think it's safe enough for me to return to Milwaukee with Chelsey?"

"I do." Slade didn't hesitate. "I wouldn't lie to you, Duncan. Not after all this." Slade reached up to rub the back of his neck. "I have to go. Thanks to that fight, there's more paperwork to complete. The locals have to report to their boss, while I have to report up to mine."

Duncan turned to face Chelsey. She stepped into his arms, wound her arms around his neck and drew him down for a kiss.

He loved kissing her and didn't want to stop, but they still needed to talk. "Chels?" he managed when he could breathe.

"Hmm?" She rested her head in the hollow of his shoulder.

"I love you and I want you to be safe."

She lifted her head, smiling at him. "I love you and want you to be safe, too. Sounds like the best option is for us to live in Milwaukee."

"Are you sure about that? About leaving the hotel behind?" He forced himself to ask the question, mentally bracing himself for her response.

"Yes, I'm sure that I want to be with you, Duncan. Even though Travis Wolfe wanted to buy the hotel, I happen to know the federal government will also be interested in taking it over, as the land is part of the Grand Teton National Park. They offered before, when my grandparents had the place."

He was humbled by how she was willing to give up her parents' home for him. "I'd like to plant a couple of trees in your parents' memory."

Her smile widened. "I'd love that."

"Chelsey, will you please marry me? I don't have a ring, but I want you to know that I love you with all my heart. I'd be honored if you'd agree to be my wife."

"Yes, Duncan, I'll marry you. I only have one request."

Anything, he thought. "Like?"

"No big fancy ceremony, just your immediate family and a few close friends. And I'd really like to be married in a church."

It was very different from what she'd planned with Brett, but he wasn't complaining. "Done. You'll like the church Shayla and Mike have taken me to. It's perfect for a small, intimate wedding ceremony."

"Good." She tugged his head down toward hers. "Please kiss me again, Duncan. Because this is the happiest day of my life."

He was more than willing to oblige her request. Because it was the happiest day of his life, too.

EPILOGUE

Four months later...

October in Wisconsin was beautiful. The blue skies were clear and the leaves on the trees were a burst of yellow, orange and red. Chelsey knew she and Duncan were blessed to have such a wonderful wedding day.

She stood in the back of the small church she'd grown to love, in a simple dress that didn't have a long train or a veil. As the organ music swelled she looked up the aisle and saw Duncan standing in a dark suit, no tux, waiting for her.

She smiled. There wasn't a single doubt in her mind or her heart about marrying Duncan O'Hare. Thankfully, their testimony against Wesley Strand had resulted in a guilty verdict. Nettles, Martin and Goldberg all agreed to plea deals. The nightmare in Wyoming was over, but the move to Milwaukee had been the right decision. She'd lived there for the first fifteen years of her life, so it was a bit like coming back home.

And there was Duncan. The most wonderful, kind, caring and compassionate man she'd ever met. He'd do anything to protect her and always followed through on his promises.

There wasn't anyone in the world like him, and she was blessed and humbled that he'd chosen her to be his wife.

The church was filled with people, more than she'd expected. But not only was the Callahan family huge and growing by the minute, there were Duncan's close friends: Hawk Jacobson, his wife Jillian, and their two kids; along with Ryker Tillman, his wife Olivia, and their two kids.

She liked how Duncan had surrounded

himself with family men. Well, except for Slade and Colt, who hung back as if afraid to be bitten by the love bug.

"Ready, Chelsey?" Per her request, Duncan's father, Ian O'Hare, was the one giving her away. Maggie Callahan O'Hare, Ian's new wife, also treated Chelsey like a daughter. She felt it was fitting for both of them to be an intricate part of their wedding and she already loved them both, very much.

Her parents would have adored them, too.

"Yes." She slid her arm through the crook of Ian's elbow and together they began their walk down the aisle toward the front of the church. At one point she must have picked up the pace because Ian whispered, "Slow down, lass, I promise he'll wait."

That made her smile. And when she caught Duncan's gaze, the love shining there was enough to bring tears to her eyes.

As Ian handed her over to Duncan, she

gave her soon-to-be father-in-law a quick hug, then clasped both Duncan's hands in hers. "I love you," she whispered.

"I love you, too," he whispered back.

Feeling secure with Duncan's and God's love surrounding them, they turned to face the pastor.

It was time to begin their new life, together.

* * * * *

If you enjoyed this book, don't miss these other stories from Laura Scott:

Shielding His Christmas Witness
The Only Witness
Christmas Amnesia
Shattered Lullaby
Primary Suspect
Protecting His Secret Son
Soldier's Christmas Secrets
Guarded by the Soldier

*Available now from
Love Inspired Suspense!*

*Find more great reads at
www.LoveInspired.com*

Dear Reader,

I hope you've enjoyed the third and final book in my Justice Seekers series. You met Hawk, Ryker and Duncan in the Callahan Confidential stories and I knew each of them deserved their own happily-ever-after. You might be happy to know I'm hard at work on another three-book series featuring—you guessed it—the US Marshals, where you are likely to meet Slade, Colt and Tanner again.

If you're interested in learning about my upcoming book releases please drop by to visit my website at www.laurascottbooks. com. Take a moment to sign up for my monthly newsletter. I offer a free and exclusive novella to all subscribers.

I adore hearing from my readers, so either drop me a note through my website, or find me on Facebook at https://www.facebook.com/LauraScottBooks/ or on Twitter at https://twitter.com/laurascottbooks.

Until next time,
Laura Scott